VEXED

By Kristy Nicolle

Queens Of Fantasy Saga
A Tidal Kiss Novella

First published by Kristy Nicolle, United Kingdom, December 2017

QUEENS OF FANTASY EDITION (1st EDITION)

Published December 2017 by Kristy Nicolle

Copyright © 2016 Kristy Nicolle

Edited By- Jaimie Cordall

Adult Paranormal/FantasyRomance

The right of Kristy Nicolle to be identified as author of this Work has been asserted by her in accordance with sections 77 and 78 of the Copyright, Designs and Patents Act 1988.

Disclaimer:

ThiS ebook is written in U.K English by personal preference of the author. This is a work of fiction. Names, characters, businesses, places, events and incidents are either the products of the author's imagination or used in a fictitious manner. Any resemblance to actual persons, living or dead, or actual events is purely coincidental.

ISBN: 978-1-911395-10-2

www.kristynicolle.com

For those of you who loved Vex from the very beginning.
Hold on to your sodding knickers,
It's time to get Vexy.

TIME FOR TEA

SOMETHING CAUSES ME TO stir from sleep; unusual for me, seeing as I hardly ever allow myself to descend into my mind's deepest recesses anymore. I find the recall of days gone past partly unsavoury, not that I can plead regret. The things I did, the blood I spilt, the skin I painted many dark colours, have long since faded and turned to dust. Yet somewhere in the back of my mind, especially now, when I'm questioning if what I am can ever truly be contained, those dark days lurk, lying in wait — tempting, to say the least.

Sitting up on the couch, I find the television blaring, some too-happy kid's movie about sisterly bonds and ice magic playing for the eighth time tonight.

I realise immediately what has woken me as I focus in on her chocolate coloured eyes, shaped like almonds and rimmed in blotchy mascara. Blinking slowly, I stare at her, taking in her painted, sticky face for a moment before I frown.

Stretching up to the ceiling as I let out a yawn, my muscles unfurl, desperate for a throat to rip out or a skull to crush. I've become far too bored sitting around being democratic lately. I think of the violence, a meek and barely forgivable distaste for it tearing me in two, making me hesitant to act at all.

"Hey, where did you get makeup from?" I demand, brushing aside the desperate oxymoron that my soul has become. She cocks her head, grinning as a dimple presents itself on the left side of her face beneath thick, badly applied blusher.

"I found it," she replies, acting dumb with a cute grin. I scrutinize her as she rearranges one of her three favourite stuffed animals atop tiny chairs, suitable for no average-sized person. They're called Geoffrey, Stan, and Theodore, though I can never remember which is which.

1

"Kayla — where did you find it *exactly*?" Leaning forward on the couch, I rest my elbows on the sharp protrusions of my knees. As Kayla moves toward the olive-green wall in front of the television, leaning against it and ignoring me, I roll my eyes.

This child.

Running my fingers back through my hair, the black locks feeling silky and dense against my fingers. I sigh, knowing I'm exhausted but also knowing that falling asleep on the job probably makes me the crappiest babysitter of all time.

The thought pains me, the idea I can't even look after myself becoming painfully evident as I drop to the floor, taking a seat with crossed legs in the free space around the tiny wooden table. The places are set for high tea, something fancy I'm sure, and I wonder why Kayla is so obsessed with tea parties. When I was a child, I was happy to sit and draw with a stick in the sand.

"Zure—" Kayla looks at me, her too large head and scrawny child's body too fragile for the cruelty of this world.

"Yes, Kayla?" I enquire as she looks between me and the television, where a blonde woman is singing about letting it go.

I suppose it's super easy to let it go when you can just freeze the ass of anyone who annoys the crap out of you. That's probably why Gideon is so chilled.

Kayla looks nervous, taking one or two steps towards me and then plopping down on the carpet in an uncoordinated mess. Her pyjamas have mermaids on them. It's her latest craze, surprising everyone— though for no good reason I can discern. Of course, she's obsessed; her entire family is bloody chosen.

Careful. I warn myself, recognising the vernacular from my least favourite person seeping into my own. The individual I quite often fantasise about beating senseless. Though, at least he's good for something these days.

"Is there really an ice city? Like, really, *really*?" she demands, voice dreamy as she cocks her head. A twinkle flickers to life behind the glassy surfaces of her eyes, making bile rise in my throat.

Her blue fuzzy pyjamas hug her as she pulls her knees up to her chest and rocks back and forth on her tailbone, looking nervous, afraid even, as I fail to reply immediately. The instantaneous change in her expression pains me, and so does the question.

Things would be so much easier if she'd just play tea party and watch the crappy movie.

"Kayla— you know I'm not allowed to talk to you about those things. Come on, let's have tea," I dismiss her. Her eyes become wider, rounder, more puppy-like as silence falls, and the wind stirs outside. The flimsy gossamer drapes flap slightly in the breeze, letting full moonlight fall uninterrupted through the pane as she sighs, tugging at the glimmer of decency left in me.

"Aww—" She's giving me that face, those innocent eyes pulling on my heartstrings, the ones I've long since discarded as flat and out of tune. I swallow, knowing in moments like this I cannot forget what I am. I cannot ignore what makes me strong but also what makes me weak. The fact that I was once a mother, but have lost the right to use such a word at my lack of presence.

"There is a city of ice. It's called the Gelida Silentium. But you know I can't tell you any more than that. And don't try those eyes on me again, or I shall cut them from your skull." The words slip from my mouth, and her eyes widen further, mouth falling slack.

I don't know where the rage has come from. I thought it disappeared along with the old order in which the Mer and Psirens had existed for so many years. I have become tired, old and cynical. Ready for it all to end.

It's not her fault, but I'm not a good, or kind, or sweet enough person to care anymore.

Perhaps I want her to hate me. Maybe, if she did, it would mean I was right all along. I am unlovable, irredeemable, and too far gone that even one so pure cannot quell my lust for bloodshed.

"Kayla, I—" I begin to apologise, heart pounding against my ribs in protest as I fear she may cry. If she does, I'll never forgive myself.

"What's wrong, Zure?" She appears unsure but gets to her feet anyway, tottering around the table on short legs and falling into my lap before glancing up at me with her clown makeup. "You seem sad," she assesses me, bringing a hand up to the locks of my hair that have fallen forward and brushing her fingers through them absentmindedly. I hold her in my arms, trying to take back what I said, trying to make her feel safe.

"I— I *am* sad." I admit, and she looks only now like she might cry.

What did I do to deserve this little girl's trust? I wonder, falling deeper into melancholy at the thought of her growing up, growing wiser, and more beautiful, growing to know that I cannot be the hero nor even the person she hopes of me.

3

"Is it because you're queen? Callie isn't sad and she's queen too," she asks me. My despair deepens.

Of course, in her eyes, the wonderful Callie Fischer should be my benchmark for lifetime achievement.

"I'm not Callie," I respond, simply grabbing her under the arms and standing her on her two feet, putting distance between us.

"No. You're better. You're stronger." Kayla assesses me yet again, and I wonder what else she thinks of me. She's astute; that's for sure. "Are you sad because you don't have a boyfriend?"

I almost laugh, finding a small smile tugging at the corners of my lips, which are so often twisted into a firm hard line these days.

"Why would you ask that?" I demand, gazing up at her and pushing my dark hair behind one ear.

"Callie has Orion— he's dreamy, and she's happy. Maybe you need someone dreamy too." Her eyes sparkle, wistful, as she does a tiny twizzle on one foot and almost loses balance. I catch her, my long dark fingernails evidently sharp against the soft milky pallor of her skin.

"I don't need a boyfriend. And if I did want one, I wouldn't want him to be dreamy," I reply, exhausted by her endless questions. I love this child, more than I had thought possible for the short amount of time I've been trusted to look after her alone. And yet, she has an insatiable curiosity unlike anything I've ever known.

"Why not?" she demands, folding her arms across the mermaid embroidered on her shirt.

I want to tell her the truth. That my dreams are all long since dead. That they died the day Poseidon and Atargatis stood before me and revealed not only my fate, but the fate of my Arabella as well.

Instead, I simply state, "Because, Kayla, not every queen needs a king to rule."

As the words leave my lips, she smiles, placing her arms around my neck and pulling me close to her still beating, innocent heart.

It's late, too late, proving yet again that I am the world's worst babysitter, when I finally get Kayla into bed. Her face has been scrubbed raw, much to her protest, but I think I finally got the majority of the world's most permanent make-up off her tiny face.

She peers up into my eyes — surrounded by Geoffrey, Stan, and Theodore — making me want to recoil, to pull away, yet I fight that urge. Her bedroom makes my stomach hurt, the pink of the walls, the gossamer of the canopy above her single bed. The way her books and toys are lovingly ragged and haphazardly stacked. It's exactly what I would have wanted for my little girl, even though back then, I never could have given her such luxuries.

"Are you good? You need a glass of water?" I ask as I pat down the duvet around her body, not wanting to sit downstairs alone. Too much time with my own thoughts is never good.

"No. I don't wanna have to potty," she informs me, yawning before rolling over under her soft pink blanket and curling up like a kitten. I stroke her hair as she closes her eyes, letting the soft silkiness of the individual strands take me away to a time that never was but could have been. To the bed of my little girl, the silken locks of Arabella, my Arabella.

As she drifts away to someplace far calmer than anywhere I'm able to reach, I get to my feet. Moving from the room as a shadow, I turn off the light and blend into the dark, into the place where Kayla's nightmares reside. Where I belong.

I descend the staircase slowly, taking each step in metronomic time, examining the family pictures that hang parallel to the wooden banister, which I brush lightly with my restless fingertips.

Smiling faces, moments captured, depictions of what I had been taken from me by a thief in the night as I had bled to death. I don't feel sad. I don't feel anything. My capacity for despair and rage is diminishing with each passing day, and I can't help but wonder if this is what dying feels like.

As I'm pondering what the end will be like, I hear the front door open, and voices erupt across the threshold as Orion, Callie, Patience, and Gideon fall into the hall, chatting with an irritating and non-infectious joviality.

"Shhh." I place my fingers to my lips and Callie immediately silences as her eyes rise to meet mine.

"Is she asleep?" she queries, hopeful, and I nod, watching as her aquamarine eyes crease at the sides with her gradual smile.

"Just about. I had a little trouble getting her to go to bed. She wouldn't stop asking me questions about certain forbidden topics." As my words ring out, cold and unfeeling, as though this issue barely affects me at all, Patience's eyes diminish. Her smile lines turn to those of worry as her eyes crease and lips purse, gaze shifting unwillingly to the landing, where they settle on Kayla's closed bedroom door.

I reach the bottom of the staircase finally, moving into the light of the hall and out of the shadow. Orion slaps his hand across his mouth, eyes bulging as he tries to stifle something that sounds like a snort. Gideon's aquamarine eyes glisten, amused, as he runs thick fingers through his braided white hair and Callie cocks her head, mystified.

What the hell is so damn funny?

"What?" I interrogate them, a severe frown marring my otherwise flawless features. Have they suddenly realised I'm flailing, falling, barely holding on? Have they finally seen my anguish? Realised I'm a joke of a ruler?

"Uh— Azure, you didn't happen to fall asleep, did you?" Patience asks, and I scowl. Her tone isn't accusatory, but rather amused as she unties her beige overcoat and slips it off.

"No. Why?"

"Why don't you hang this up for me over there." She passes me her coat, and I debate throwing it back at her, yet something about Callie's mother makes me feel inferior. Though, whether it's because she's done what I could not or because she reminds me of my own mother and her inescapable maternal warmth, I don't know.

I step off the bottom stair, twisting on the ball of my foot and striding toward a standing coat rack in front of a large wide mirror, hanging on the wall opposite the staircase.

As I place the overcoat on the hook and turn back in haste, something about my appearance catches my eye.

I stall, pivoting back in slow motion to examine myself in the puddle of reflective glass.

Crap.

Kayla has plastered thick jammy make-up all over my pale complexion, slathering me in pink glittery eyeshadow and bright red lipstick which twists my mouth into a sick half-smile, half-grimace. My cheeks look like those of a circus clown, rosy and thick with blusher.

This child. I cuss again internally, watching as the foursome bursts into full-blown laughter at my expense. I know I should laugh too, should live in the moment, but for some reason, this all seems way beyond what I deserve. A happy family, a laughing family, a blessed family.

This is so not my freaking look.

I

A DANGEROUS GAME

THE SHADOWS OF THE eight separate Alcazars fall upon the stark monochrome of the courtyard central to The Occulta Mirum. My tailfin slices through the water with slow ease, even though I'm running late.

I know only too well by now that I have absolutely no desire to give in to the spectacle I'm about to witness. Yet I'm still swimming forward, a clockwork toy with no choice but to obey the unstoppable turning key so cruelly embedded in its spine.

"Azure." Orion acknowledges my arrival, looking increasingly nervous as I propel toward the centre of the courtyard. The symbol of the circle of eight — four overlapping crescent moons surrounding the number itself — lies embedded into the ground, a permanent and unending reminder of what has passed. Not that I need it.

Eight golden statues depicting Poseidon, Atargatis, Ava, Neptune, Kanaloa, Mizuchi, Sena, and Lir also surround my brother as he stares wearily at my sullen face. I exhale, a flurry of bubbles rising in front of my face to tickle my forehead, putting me more on edge.

"Best get this over with, then. I want it noted that I told you this was a terrible idea," I complain, folding my arms over the untarnished black of my breast scales as I right myself in the water.

I feel the slits of my gills open and close, heartbeat heavy and torturous as dread floods my stomach.

"Noted," he sighs, mouth falling into a firm unamused line.

"Where's Blondie?" I ask him, utilising Vex's nickname for Callie without a second thought. He shifts in the water, visibly relaxed now I've changed the subject. His royal blue tailfin undulates beneath the disgustingly muscular lines that track down his torso, falling into scale as he inhales, smiling.

8

"She's at the game already. Wanted to arrive before the other council members. After all, we both knew you'd be late." He gives me a sly glance, like he's got me all figured out as we swim, side by side, toward the arena.

"You see, if this was a *good* idea, she wouldn't need to babysit the rest of the stupid council," I mutter, and Orion rolls his eyes.

"Look, I get it—you're scared. If Poseidon had threatened me the way he did you, I would be too, but we can't just keep them locked up. You've said that before. It's about integration, right?" He's trying to be reasonable, sweet even, making me want to smack him in his stupidly perfect face.

I think back to the night Starlet passed, how I'd beaten him black and blue.

Good times. I muse as we pass under the shadows of the farthest Alcazars, belonging to the Kappa and Sirena, in bloody scarlet and hideous fuchsia pink.

The sky overhead is grey, and the water is reflective; a still, black mirror for the world above, at least for now. It looks like a storm is brewing, perfectly resonant of my current mood.

"I said integrate, not throw them into the deep end with freaking contact sports," I snort, shaking my head so my dark hair billows out in the surrounding water, noxious, as my pupils dilate.

"They were born in the deep end. Besides, don't you think it's more likely that this is something they'll excel at? I don't see them wanting to get involved in ocean conservation, do you?" Orion asks as we pass rows upon rows of glistening surface scrapers. The bottles embedded into their walls are whole again, a far cry from when they had been shattered and jagged under Psiren rule.

"Does drowning sailors count?" I ask him, a wicked smile tilting the corners of my grim lips. Orion doesn't look impressed, cocking his head at me with a serious gaze.

"That's not funny."

"It's funny if you're me," I retort, and he runs his hand back through his hair, frustrated. I roll my eyes. "Look, I was put in charge of these rabid teenagers, okay? If shit goes wrong, I'm the one getting dragged to hell, not you. I know this darkness better than anyone, and I think this is a stupid idea. Just because Domnall wants a freaking fight because he's bored isn't a reason to throw the Psirens into something like this. Besides, Isabella seemed rather up for the idea. I think it's a setup," I admit, biting my bottom lip and balling my fists at my sides as

I increase pace. My hair is pushed flat against my skull now as Orion surges forward, catching up to me in only seconds. He looks outraged.

"That's ridiculous; Isabella wouldn't do that." Orion stands up for her, and I cock an eyebrow in disbelief.

"Seriously? I mean, how stupid are you, Orion? She hates the Psirens. Though I can't discern why. They killed her asshole ex-husband. She should be thanking them." I'm indignant, and Orion blinks a few times, taking in what I've said like I'm speaking a foreign language.

"Why do you do that? Lash out when you're scared?" he demands, the new Hydraball stadium towering over us as we approach the enormity of its jade, crystalline height.

"I'm not scared. I'm fucking pissed!" I yell, losing my temper as I wonder when he got so insanely dense.

"You don't seem pissed to me. You seem—" he begins, and I cut him off.

"How? How do I *seem* to you, oh mighty Orion?" I snap. He shakes his head, eyes narrowing as his gaze becomes firm. His biceps bulge as he rights himself in the water, folding them across his chest and exhaling heavily, angry.

"You seem freaking suicidal. Like you don't care. You could've stopped this. If you had come to Callie and me, given us good reasons, we would have listened. Instead, you just—" he's stuttering, trying to put the blame on me like the coward he is.

"Just *what* exactly?" I bark, only marginally avoiding hissing at him.

"You rolled over. You gave in," he informs me. I snort.

"No shit. I didn't ask for this job. And nobody wants me to have it or respects my right to it. Not the Psirens, not the council, not you. I'm just the weird girl in the corner with the bad attitude who got the shit stick because some God said so!" I spit, moving to swim away, to avoid any conflict that may put my self-restraint at risk of failure. I'm so done with this conversation, with him. He doesn't know me any more than our father did after all those years we spent apart.

"Azure—" he calls after me, and I turn, momentarily hoping more than anything that he'll call this off, that he'll tell me he thinks I can do this. That he knows I have what it takes and that I'm right.

"It'll all be fine," he simply says as the flurry of bubbles around me disperses, letting his frail blue gaze drop from mine.

Coward. I growl inwardly.

"For the Selkies' sakes, I hope you're right," I call back over my shoulder, proceeding to the inside of the stadium and not looking back.

"You're late," Callie notes as I drift into the royal box, taking several strokes through the water and emerging from behind her makeshift throne. I take a seat on a similar throne to her left, between her and Callista. Baby pink sandstone surrounds us on all sides, separating us from the rest of the crowd, those who remain inferior to us through no fault of their own.

The young mermaid queen's blonde hair and aqua fluke sparkle unnaturally bright for such a dull day, causing something within my gut to grate like two pieces of broken glass being rubbed together.

"That would be because I didn't want to come," I retort with a deadpan expression. Callie places a hand on mine as I let my palm fall to the armrest of the black crystal chair, as though it's comfort I want and not to be heeded.

"It'll be fine. I don't know why you're so worried," she tries to assure me, essentially repeating the words of her soulmate, to no avail. I pull my hand from beneath hers and sit back in my throne, looking dead ahead and not replying as I contemplate why I bothered coming at all. As if I need to witness my own failings in person. She has no clue what she's doing, but because she had a small brush with the darkness, it's like suddenly she's an expert.

Pffft. I sneer internally. *I've seen lattes darker than her soul.*

"All will be well, Azure." Callista tries to comfort me too, again repeating the same sentiment as everyone else, but I have no use for her hopeful attitude either. Her zebra striped tailfin remains eerily still in the water as I grit my teeth, ignoring her too. She irritates me, but I don't turn to her, despite the audible clicking of her shell-beaded braids continuing to grind against my rapidly fraying temper. Instead, I choose to be ignorant to the world around me, a most pleasant state to be sure.

I look down at the charred scales on my tailfin, at the way they bind me to the ocean in the worst way possible. They shackle me to its darkness, to its hate, its destruction.

The water above is twisting into silvery clouds, heavy like liquid mercury, reflecting the silent fury of my temper. It remains trapped and useless behind my fear and hesitation to act, an invisible threat to all.

I stare at Callie for a second, remembering her with black hair and dark eyes. She suffered with the temptation for mere days. Until you've been in that shadow for several centuries, torn skin from muscle and tissue from bone with a smile on your face, you don't get to tell me shit about darkness.

I curl my fluke, impatient, flexing my muscles and trying to distract myself as a deep sound echoes out through the water, pulling my attention to the centre of the stadium.

Gideon's lips are wrapped around the end of a large, pink conch shell, his expansive chest exhaling air to signal the game is about to get underway. I take this opportunity to lean forward, wondering how entertaining this slow-motion car wreck will turn out to be.

In the too-bright stands of the tall cylindrical stadium, Psirens are already cat-calling Mermaids on the opposing side of the circular seating arrangements. I watch as Isabella, three seats down from me on the right, rolls her eyes and grimaces in distaste.

As if Paolo wasn't just as bad, and he didn't have dark, potent magic as an excuse.

"Welcome, Kindred, to the first official game of the Hydraball season! We have one hell of a match today with the Psirens of The Deep versus the Selkies of Scotland!" Gideon bellows, the white of his tail stark in the dim light as the brewing storm builds into a furious tumult overhead.

The crowd cheers, deafening, as a flash of lightning sparks above the ferocity of the surface. Thunder surely follows, but is drowned out by bloodthirsty screams from the surrounding fans.

My gaze finds Domnall in the din, his fiery red hair and enormous mass difficult to ignore. He looks contented, relaxed even, cocky. I find this ironic, because it was only recently the Psirens had nearly ripped him limb from limb. Though, seemingly, despite the unrest and prejudice, the council appears to have forgotten just how dangerous those with my persuasion can be. Or, at least, enough not to take me seriously in the slightest.

The teams emerge from the dark tunnels that lead from the outside of the stadium to the central playing space, which hangs vertically, with only green sand marking it as any different from any other patch of ocean.

I am glad, at this moment, for the saving grace that is the size of the opposing team. The Selkies are by far the savviest warriors of all the Mer pods. With their thick dumb accents and ridiculous muscles, they are little more than biceps with a brain attached, if you ask me. At least, though, they'll have a chance of fighting back.

Behind them, a swarm of Psirens takes to the arena, their oddly mismatched bodies and pale skin unmistakable. As they zoom forward to take their starting positions, ready for Gideon to begin the match as referee, I hear booing from the crowd. My heart sinks.

I don't give a shit about the Psirens, but that's just uncalled for. This is supposed to be about moving on. I shake my head, but don't rise to object or call for silence.

In days gone by, I would have ripped out the throat of anyone who crossed me or those in my protection, but as of now, I am tired. Exhausted. The Psirens barely respect me as a leader, so it's almost impossible to imagine why the other Mer pods would. Then again, what did I expect? They didn't choose me. They chose Solustus and loved Alyssa as a mother; I'm nothing but a murderer to them.

Oh, the irony.

I was a fighter, but that part of me is fading to nothing but memory, leaving only harsh words and little action in its stead.

Gideon calls for silence, with noticeable irritation in his tone, causing the crowd to stir as I take in the team that Vex has put together. He's the captain, hanging in the water with undulating tentacles attached to his infuriatingly hard abs. He's netter for the team, which has caused nothing but issues from day one. I swear, the time I've spent having arguments over the advantage of his tentacles when defending the Psiren's goal is just plain ridiculous. It's not like I don't have better stuff to do. Like, for example, loathing him from afar and avoiding the mere memory of our encounter in the corner of my throne room. Or plotting his death while imagining the many ways in which I might maim him if I had the energy or inclination.

As it is, I've decided he's not even worth the effort violence requires, so I merely seethe in silence with narrow, dark eyes from a distance. Letting my hate turn my bitter heart even colder.

I examine the rest of the team as they take their places in the water, muscles visibly tense as eyes dilate dark, making even me increasingly uneasy.

Celius, the most volatile of the group, reminding me ever so slightly of Caedes in his temperament, is one of the four interceptors. Unfortunately, he's not as spindled in figure as Caedes, with bulging muscles and a torso thick with masculine power. His tail is that of a barracuda, agile and dangerous, and his cropped hair is like bloody seaweed as it floats incrementally in the surrounding water.

I should probably know the names of the other interceptors, yet I don't.

I know Darius is the slingshot, having boasted to me about his experience in high school football because that's absolutely the same thing.

Not.

Other than this, I know nothing of how the game will unfold, or even the intricacies of how it's played.

Orion tried to explain it to me a dozen times, but just as my sister had thought it pointless, so do I. Netters defend the hoops at the top of the arena, anchors remain in the bottom quarter, stopping the heavy pearlescent ball from hitting the green sand below, interceptors fight for possession, and the slingshots in the upper-mid section of the vertical arena shoot past the netters for points. Or that's essentially what I picked up from the seven-hour conversation Orion had torturously forced me into.

It's like they're all looking for a way to relate to the Psirens, rather than viewing them as a different animal entirely. Domestication is the goal, like a proud lion made to perform in a circus. It makes me sick. Not that it should. It's not like I have any better ideas on how to harness the Psirens or their dark power.

The game begins as another sound passes through the body of the conch and into the stormy grey of the water. I sit back in my seat, waiting for the crash and burn, which I know is inevitable.

God, this is boring. I muse, wishing now that some kind of violent altercation would break out. It's all very artistic, the way they throw their bodies through the water, slapping hard, dense tailfin against the ball. But what the hell is the point? It's a complete waste of time and effort.

The Psirens have behaved themselves, without so much as a penalty so far, and I watch Gideon like a hawk as he continues to judge the state of play. Aedan, one of the interceptors for the Selkies, comes close to me. So near, in fact, that I feel the surrounding fluid displace from his course through the water as I hang, listless, over the partition of the royal box, half-heartedly pondering whether to toss myself over the edge.

The other leaders are sitting, backs straight, and two in particular look somewhat irritated. I assume because my people haven't yet mass murdered the entire ginger squad opposing them. I turn back, watching as Aedan maintains possession of the ball, sighing out as my boredom reaches its underwhelming peak.

As the bubbles clear from my vision, Celius comes up the inside of Aedan's track but can't keep pace as the enormous muscles of his opponent outreach his swimming capabilities.

Weenie. I think.

My eyes widen as I see it.

Something in his eyes, something I've seen before in the mirror.

Malice.

Celius reaches out, closing the gap between himself and Aedan, grabbing the Selkie's red hair in his palms and pulling him toward him with a jerk. His forehead cracks audibly against the man's skull as he headbutts him and takes the ball. His eyes are fully dilated as he turns to me, and Aedan sinks to the floor. I perk up, righting myself as Gideon blows on the conch shell, and the arena explodes into outrage.

I watch as Aedan regains his composure, stopping his descent toward the seabed. Within moments, he and Celius are soaring through the water, a sick, twisted tornado of cracking bones and flashing teeth. Celius' skin maps dark with power, and I merely float, dead inside, watching as the council rises in hurried unison from their thrones. I catch Vex descending from above with an audible, yet predictable, "Bloody hell!" escaping his lips.

The scrapping pair crashes to the floor, and several of the Psiren players look at me. I hang, unimpressed, as a mushroom cloud of green sand flies upward in the water. The ball falls to the floor beside them, play forgotten.

The crowd does something unexpected, descending from the stands and piling into the space of the arena, packing it shoulder to shoulder with bodies as they watch the brawl with fascination from above. Trapping the fighters in on all sides, most of them, unsurprisingly, are egging on Aedan. The Psirens look like they might get involved, their eyes turning dark in unison as they stare up at me, like I'm a dark sun. As though I'm there to stop them, to burn them to a cinder for breaking the rules. I do nothing.

Callie and Orion fight their way through the crowd with the rest of the leaders in tow as lightning flashes overhead, illuminating lime sand hanging like synthetic poison, even at this height in the water.

15

I watch on, unmoved to act.

After a few moments of being on the outside, squinting down upon the spectacle, I find Gideon and Vex at the centre of it all, each one restraining a bloody, bruised figure.

Celius' wild eyes stare up at me from the ground like a naughty child as he licks his lower lip. It's spattered with Aedan's blood.

I told you this was a bad idea, is the only thought I can form, expression dead on my face as rigor mortis settles comfortably over my soul.

"Azure!" Isabella calls out, rising in the water. "What do you have to say to this — this *monster*?" She demands an answer from me, the rubies of her tail catching the light in gory splendour. Her dark hair is luscious around her face, beauteous, but her dark eyes are vindictive and laced with predictably sour intent. The crowd lifts its collective gaze to me as I stare at Orion, the expression not angry but simply dissonant.

"Yes, Azure, you really should deal with this," Callie prompts me, rising in front of Isabella as if to shield me from the viciousness of her gaze. She has kindness in her eyes, more than I deserve, especially from the likes of her oh-so-blessed self.

I exhale silently, staring down, yet again, upon my people. I pick out Vex in the crowd, hating him all the more for the way his eyes are imploring me to speak, to say something, anything.

With this, I turn, rising into the metallic fury of the storm overhead. Letting it carry me back to the Dark Alcazar, lightning illuminating only the lifelessness within my eyes.

Later, floating on the balcony of my suite in the Dark Alcazar, I look up at the now still waters. The sun is poking between dark clouds, leaving a shadow limned, golden light falling over the city. Perhaps that's why everyone expects me to move forward from the darkness back to light; because in the natural world, the rebirth of life in spring so naturally follows the death of fall and winter. The problem with that analogy is that by equating the Psirens to something natural, you are dismissing the truth. We are not natural. We are abominations, created to kill and not to feel. The ultimate weapon, and yet one with such destructive power, even the god who created it cannot contain.

So, now that's my job.

Yippee. I roll my eyes, folding my arms across my breast scales and exhaling a stream of bubbles. The dark crystal railing of the suite matches the rest of the décor as it climbs in finely carved tentacles from the floor, twisting around itself to form a thick and intimidating border between me and fluid infinity.

Gazing down over the city, I see the Psirens; noticeable because of their speed and motion, far greater and more rabid than the others. They're young, fresh, and energetic, but they don't respect me, and I don't respect them. I have no power over them, and any power I thought I had was dismissed as merely a figment of my imagination when Atargatis and Poseidon gave me this job against my consent.

I hear a knock at the door but don't answer. I want to be alone. If I wanted to socialise, I'd have stayed at the stadium.

I spin away from the balcony, wanting to avoid people knowing my whereabouts, and close the two glass doors leading outward behind me as I slash through the water.

Inside my suite, a black crystal four poster bed, designed to look like it's being supported entirely by yet more tentacles, is central to the space. Heavy, black velvet sheets lie bound to the mattress. It's unfortunate, because every single night as I lay down to sleep, I picture him, his velvety clutch, the shadows cast by the four tentacle-shaped posts of the frame serving as a constant fucking reminder of him and everything I love to hate. The headboard is encrusted with bloody rubies and black onyx, backlit with blue algae, and emits a bizarre, lilac glow throughout the space. I hang in shadows cast by the black crystal walls as another and more persistent knock comes ringing through the water.

I freeze as the door at the far end of the room slowly opens. Vex lets himself in.

"How polite of you to break and enter on my behalf," I snap. He jumps, eyes moving to my silhouette, statuesque in the dark.

"Bloody hell! You scared the shit out of me!" he complains. I snort.

"That's what happens when you're caught red-handed being a prize dick," I retort. His eyes glisten, the lilac of their depths only highlighted by the glow from the headboard.

"I'm following orders. Nothing more, love," he insists. I roll my eyes again, wondering why he even bothers pretending he doesn't seek me out just to annoy me.

"Don't you find it funny that we're the ones following orders, and yet we're also the ones they're so afraid of?" I ask, earnest. He shrugs, the rounded musculature of his shoulders rising and falling in the water. His tentacles undulate, pushing him incrementally toward me, slowly, like he hopes I won't notice.

"I never really thought about it, love. Besides, I can't be arsed getting into political drama; it's really not my scene. Callie and Orion want to see you. Unsurprisingly."

"Great," I exhale, and Vex pulsates closer yet again, the ridges of his chest muscles defined in the dark as light plays tricks with his razor-sharp cheekbones.

"You alright, love. You seem—" he begins, but I cut him off.

"I don't care how I seem to you."

"Right. Well then, you'd better get going. I'm gonna just sit here until you leave. I'm not suffering the scorn of that blonde twiglet for being a crappy messenger boy." He shoos me from my room, and I scowl. I want to beat him senseless, to gain proximity so I can rip his too smooth skin into more satisfying shreds, yet I'm scared of that kind of closeness when it comes to him.

He's dangerous.

"So, let me get this straight — my choices are hang out with a tentacled asshole, or hang out with a council of six very *official* dumbasses?" I glare at him, gritting my teeth and balling my fists at my side. As I clench my biceps, I let the tension leave me at the sudden recollection that Vex just isn't worth the effort. None of this is.

I rotate in the water to swim away, but Vex calls after me.

"Hey! I'm more bloody fun than those dumbasses any day, and if you'd just be honest with yourself, you'd admit that!"

I don't give him the courtesy of a response.

In the boardroom with the Council of Eight, or seven, with Vex's convenient and welcome absence, the chosen of the Gods and Goddesses stare at me with disapproval. I sit back in my chair, facing the round crystal table, flick my tailfin restlessly, and stare at each of them with dead, bored eyes.

"So, I'm pretty sure we can say that today's game was a disaster." Callie states the freaking obvious, and I scowl, my entire face transformed with disdain.

"Oh, really? I thought it was going so well, what with the beating people senseless. My mistake."

"Azure—" Orion interjects, and I cock my head. Not getting angry as I usually would, but sighing.

"I told you it was a bad idea. I said that. Several times. Does everyone here recall the many *hundreds* of times I have already said this? Or do you all have short-term memory loss? I mean, I know I'm a seer, but a blind monkey with a short-range periscope could have seen this shit coming." I glare at them, and Isabella rises in her chair.

Here we fucking go.

"Azure, I have given you a chance, but you are not fit to rule these creatures. Perhaps — perhaps, darling, that is not all on you. I do not believe they can be controlled. I have said this from the very beginning." She informs me of her oh-so-important opinion as Domnall stirs in his seat, taking her hand in his. I watch his tattoos bulge and whirl on his enormous biceps, rage too visible.

I narrow my eyes. Her husband hasn't been sand two months. Though, that said, he was also an asshole. Match made in freaking heaven, right?

"And yet here we are, sitting and having a civilised conversation, while I'm distinctly *not* ripping your head from your body," I remind her with a sigh, staring at my nails without care as Domnall rises in the water.

"Ah dornt appreciate ye talkin' tae mah hen loch 'at." His voice comes out as a growl, his long red braid dangling down over his shoulder as he places both hands down on the table and bears forward like a pissed off grizzly bear.

"Subtitles please?" I cock my head. Kaiya speaks up next.

"You shouldn't disrespect Isabella like that. She's far worthier of a say than *you*," she spits, still grief-stricken over the loss of Akachi, the chief of the Maneli.

"That's the problem, though, isn't it? If you would all stop being a bunch of prejudiced assholes, you'd have listened to me. You're happy to put the blame on me for this, and yet, as I recall, I was the one who saw this coming. As I have already said. You just don't want to admit you're fucking wrong and that you need me to make this little problem go away," I press them, trying to find strength despite my lack of desire.

The group looks at me with majority distaste as I lean back in the cold hard clutch of my seat and cross my arms, unfeeling.

"I think it might be best if Orion and I speak with Azure alone on this matter," Callie announces. Gideon nods, shifting in his seat to leave. Cage, the vessel for Sedna, rises to follow him, and yet the others, including the Sirena of Hawaii, don't look appeased.

"Of course you do. You'll just let her off the hook. You always do. She gets away with more than any of us," Casmire snarls, shooting me a judgemental and heated gaze.

Callie's eyes widen.

"Get out!" she decrees, raising her voice and grabbing onto Orion's arm in warning. I know what she intends to do, because I've had it done to me before. She fully expects to have to absorb Orion's power over air and clear the room herself. Instead, knowing that this is a fight they can't win, the rest of the council rises, the multiple hues of each individual tail glistening as they sway from left to right in their wakes.

The double doors close behind them, and Callie takes her seat once again, looking at me with a concerned expression.

"Look, you're right. We didn't listen. But you didn't exactly fight for your opinion either. Are you okay? You just seem — "

What is this? Analyse Azure day? I muse, realising she's the third person in as many hours to question my mental state, like it's any of her damn business.

"What? Like I don't give a damn?" I finish the sentence for her, and she nods, lips pursing as her brow furrows. Orion watches me with a cold expression, curiosity or concern — I can't tell which — flickering behind the glacial blue of his irises. I wonder what he's thinking before losing the ability to care.

"Well, yes, exactly like that," Callie agrees. I rise in my seat, clearing my throat.

"I don't. I don't care anymore." I shrug, flipping my hair over one shoulder and moving to leave.

"Wait. Azure, what do you want to do about Celius?" she calls after me, desperate and exasperated. I twist back, dark hair shrouding me as I flash her a pissed off gaze over one shoulder.

"Whatever you want. You're a better queen than I'll ever be, anyway."

2

THE DIRTY TOUR GUIDE

I SWIM THROUGH THE high arch of the aquamarine crystal doors and out into the corridor, ignoring the calls of Callie and Orion that follow.

"That's not true, you know." His voice catches me off guard, and I discover that I'm affected by what I've just said more than I realise. I've swum right past the lurking, tentacular asshole without even registering he's there.

"Jesus, you stalker! Go away." Vex inches closer to me from the shadow in which he's cloaked, bubbles rising around him as his tentacles sway back and forth. His eyes glint lilac as he moves into the light.

"I need to talk to you." He gets that face, the one I see every time he tries to corner me to 'talk'. It's been going on ever since the night of Callie and Orion's wedding, and I'm getting beyond sick of it.

He wants to talk about the kiss. The kiss in the throne room. But I have no desire to throw up in my mouth, and so have been avoiding him at all costs.

Turning from him, I flex my tailfin, swimming away and tensing my muscles as I make a bolt for the main entrance of the Alcazar.

Who knew being queen could be this much fun?

I hear him approaching behind me as I hit the courtyard.

What — did he not get the hint that I want nothing to do with him? Was my desperate effort to flee not clear enough?

"Bloody just wait, Azure!" he exclaims, and I shake my head.

Is he insane? I wonder momentarily, not pausing to entertain him.

A local group of Mer and a handful of Adaro warriors turn to us, and I realise Vex is on the verge of causing a scene. If he blurts we kissed, I swear to God I'm going to murder him where he floats with my bare hands. That is not something I will ever be able to live down, and with my luck, I still have a long freaking life ahead of me.

"*WHAT?*" I turn, yelling in his face and grabbing him by the elbow. I yank him behind me, slashing through the water and ordering the two Psiren guards to open the double doors to the Dark Alcazar. It envelops us as we pass through, rising high through dark, faceted crystal on all sides.

I clench my bicep once I'm inside, throwing Vex to the floor. "What the fuck is wrong with you? Yes, we kissed, okay? Get the fuck over it! You don't even mean anything to me. You're just some asshole who I can't seem to get rid of!" I exclaim, anger rising to the surface for the first time in what seems like forever. What is it about him that gets right under my skin, makes my blood boil, and my heart race?

Fucker.

He lurches from the floor, flying toward me and gripping the tops of my arms in his large, rough palms, squeezing hard. His eyes dilate to abyssal black, reflecting my own pissed off expression right back at me.

"Alright, love, we're just going to have to do this the hard way. If you don't want to hear about your daughter, which I think you sorely bloody need right now, then so be it. I'll just piss off, and you can go back to being Queen Bitch of the seven seas, alone!" He yells this in my face, and I feel it drain of any colour from my prior outburst. My heart goes cold, dead in my chest, faltering in its torturously unending beat.

Vex spins, tentacles flaring out from his waist as he releases me from his fraught grasp. As he does so, I become suddenly desperate, clawing forward through the water and rushing to place my fingertips on the back of his shoulder. He glances back, eyes sparking with triumph, flashing as they take in my plea.

"What do you mean, my daughter?" I whisper, having lost the power in my voice. Yet again, the prospect of Arabella, even the mere mention of her, has quelled my anger, my hate, my darkness.

"Oh, so now she's all interested—" Vex gets a sly smile, and I raise my hand in the water, the inclination to slap him seven ways from Sunday overpowering me. He grabs my wrist, coming close as his tentacles wrap around the free hand that still hangs, clenched into a fist. "Uh, uh, uh..." His lips purse, the hard edges of his cheekbones protruding as he sucks in water, and his nostrils flare, aroused.

I tilt my head, exposing my face from beneath the dark curtain of my hair, and allow my pupils to dilate.

"As your queen, I demand you tell me," I decree, putting on the fiercest voice I can manage. His tentacles still in the water, and he comes in closer, placing his lips against the shell of my ear. I fight the urge to bite the side of his face, ending him right here and now with the swift snap of his neck. Internal decapitation has always been one of my specialties.

"You're not *my* queen, love. I'm the vessel of Poseidon, in case you've forgotten. I don't answer to anyone, let alone you. At least, not while we're outside the bedroom—" he cocks his slit eyebrow, pulling back once more and shooting me a suggestive look as he goes. I exhale.

"Pig."

"Bitch."

We float at a crossroads, neither of us moving, caught together in a moment of stalemate. His proximity to me makes my rage flare, the part of me I feel I have lost momentarily returning.

Why is it he brings out the worst in me?

"What do you want?" I demand, cocking my head as he relinquishes his grip on me. Gently dipping in the water, my body relaxes more than it has in days.

"I want you to talk to me. That's all," he replies, and I turn surprised as I remain close to him despite my overwhelming instinct to flee.

"That's it?" I ask, wondering what the catch is. Crossing my arms, defensive even still, my suspicion refuses to cease. I flick my tailfin as he nods.

I hear whispers coming from beyond the closed doors behind us, the dim outlines of the guards moving behind the thick partial transparency of the crystal. I glower and wish they would turn to sand where they're immersed.

Is it normal for a queen to wish death upon her subjects so freely? I wonder.

"Come on. Let's go somewhere more private," I bite, grabbing his wrist and pulling him along beside me as I rise through the building's central hollow column, ascending in continual and effortless momentum. The dark crystal spirals around us create a barren shell of crisp, sharp shadow and many places to hide. The space is cast in dim blue light, and as the water runs over my skin, silken and cold, I hear Vex reply, "I thought you'd never ask, love."

Ignoring him, I continue along my path through the Alcazar, keeping up momentum as we pass down long and labyrinthine corridors until we reach the onyx doors of my chambers. I chose this room because it's the furthest from any other, not because it's the biggest or most luxurious by any standard. I guess that tells you where my priorities lie these days.

Inside, I position myself to the left of the door, letting Vex into my personal space before I close it behind him. Being the animal I am, I know how to make sure I have my escape route.

Pivoting, I right myself so I'm erected with a single flick of my charred tailfin, staring at him with high expectation. He watches me for a few moments, like he's uncomfortable or waiting for something. We both float, silent.

"Well?" I shake my head, rolling my eyes and clicking my tongue against the roof of my mouth. Suddenly, he seems nervous, fumbling as he rubs his palms down the front of his body like they're sweaty.

"Uh, oh — right, well, when we had that kiss in the throne room before, I saw the memories that Atargatis gave you," he announces. I feel kind of violated.

"Is that it?!" I snap, relaxing back into my Psiren persona, momentarily abandoning the weak queen in chains I've become.

"Not exactly. The grave, the location where she's buried. I know where it is, love. So, I thought I should tell you." He looks so earnest, a weird expression on him, and my eyes narrow.

"You've known this all along, and you're only just telling me now?" I accuse him, temper threatening to overwhelm me as I tense my jaw.

"Hey, I tried! You shoved bloody wedding cake in my face!" he exclaims. I snort.

"And the month between then and now? What about that? It just — slipped your mind, I suppose?" My lips purse, and I suck in my cheeks, biting down hard on the inside of my mouth as a fire ignites within my chest. I clench my fists as they drop to my sides.

"What? You mean I was supposed to know that avoiding me and locking yourself away in this place was some secret female signal for 'Oh pursue me! Bloody pursue me, Vex!'" His voice goes high pitched, mocking me as he flutters his lashes and brings his hands up like he might swoon. The urge to beat the crap out of him increases considerably.

"You were supposed to be honest. Why didn't you tell me right away?" I demand, and he scowls yet again.

"You shoved me to the ground and told me to get the hell out of your throne room! What is that? More fucking woman code I was supposed to decipher? I'm not a bloody mind reader!"

"Well, apparently you freaking are!" I retort, heart pounding in my chest, exciting me. This is the first time I've felt anything since that kiss all those weeks ago, and I'm beginning to hate myself for it.

We fall into silence, and the corners of my lips twitch. I almost want to smile at the ridiculousness of this situation and yet refuse to let Vex see I'm not pissed. Torturing him this way is far too much fun.

"What do you want me to do with this information, exactly?" I query, wondering what his motives are.

"I thought I'd take you there if you like, love. Seems like you could use some closure to me." I gape at his reply.

So, what, he's doing this because he *cares*? That seems about as likely as Isabella awarding me the Nobel peace prize.

"Why don't you just tell me where it is?" I demand, and his eyes narrow.

"What — you don't think you'll need a tour guide going all the way to England?" he asks, and my eyes widen.

England? How did my Arabella end up there? I wonder, mind immediately latching onto the information.

"Even if I needed a tour guide, I wouldn't want one as disgusting as you. It's a sensitive matter, as I'm sure you can imagine, and I don't need you tainting everything with your filthy mouth." I want the words to hurt him, so he leaves and doesn't come back, but instead, a small glint grows behind his eye, pissing me off. "You can go now," I bark, sick of the sight of him.

I turn, opening the door for him and watching as he comes closer. My skin heats slightly as he licks his bottom lip.

"*Thanks so much for the information, Vex. You're my bloody hero.*" He mocks me again in a high-pitched voice, and I glare at him as he passes.

"I don't want anyone knowing what you just told me. Keep it to your damn self, alright?" I warn him, ushering him out as fast as I can.

"And if I go running to Callie and Mr. Onion?" he asks, a sly and dangerous smile stretching his lips wide.

I could threaten him or play into his game whereby he baits, and I bite, causing him pleasure beyond what he deserves.

Instead of satiating his lust for fraught discourse, though, I slam the door in his face before turning and sliding down the length of it, defeated. I sit on the oil-slick black stone of the floor, tail outstretched before me, running my fingers through my long black hair. I'm trying to absorb the information that my daughter ended up in England, and in this process, I can't help but ask the question.

Of all the goddamn places, why there?

I stare up at the ceiling, breathing in and out as I lay splayed among the velvet of the sheets.

I let my fingers crawl through them, crablike as they elongate, spindled. The sensation of the fabric on my skin is one of pleasurable distaste, much like all experiences with Vex, and I wonder now why that is. I don't want to admit it, and yet, I cannot deny that arguing with him is the only thing that makes me feel truly alive these days.

Is it because I have unresolved issues with my daughter? Is that why I seem to look over each passing moment of my life as a spectator rather than an active participant?

Perhaps.

But what would standing where her body lies beneath as bone and dust achieve?

Probably nothing.

I hadn't expected to survive the last battle with the Psirens; maybe I hadn't wanted to either. Despite this, though, what I couldn't have seen coming was what actually happened. Being charged with the care and restraint of the Psirens when I can barely restrain myself, or at least, that was before. Now it seems only a certain tentacled asshat can rekindle the fire within my chest, the raging storm that has eroded my small and shrivelled heart.

Perhaps the worst part of all of this is that I have no tangible target for my rage, and maybe that's why I'm so angry with Vex and yet physically dissonant with everyone else. He embodied the god that cursed me this way, bestowed more responsibility than I could ever imagine, nor have ever desired. Now Poseidon is gone, up in The Higher Plains, and I'm left here, stuck. They also gave me some semblance of what they deem a reward. Fractured memories from the life of my daughter which did not give me the comfort I imagined but merely left me more disconnected from her memory, realising that her life is long over, long gone.

I, of course, have always known this somewhere in the back of my mind, but I have never accepted it. Maybe I've always hoped some mystical force would keep her alive until we could one day be reunited, and I could say everything I've always dreamed of. But as it is, her life passed too fast, cruelly fast, and I never had the chance to say hello, let alone goodbye.

I sigh out, pondering the possibility of a journey to England.

Will it help or hurt?

The lilac glow of the algae shining out from behind the red crystal facets of the headboard blankets me, and I close my eyes, remembering her tiny body. The weight of it in my arms, her smell, the way her fingers had grabbed mine moments before I had bled to death.

Then it occurs to me that maybe I don't know enough. Had my husband given her a good life? Or had she become downtrodden, just like my sister had before she was chosen? I would have taught her to be strong, to be a fighter. Just like me, or— just like I was.

I let my head loll to the side and stare at the vanity in the corner of the room. It's made from azure crystal, the legs looking like that of an eerie crustacean. Crystal instruments of beauteous torture lie atop the slick surface. A too sharp comb, made from the remnants of a dead swordfish, catches my eye in particular.

I see the mirror from afar, my face blurred from this distance, and imagine it's her face. I would sit her down and brush her hair, ask her about her day, about her life.

The notion of what could have been is too painful to maintain, and so I let the vision dissipate like rain upon the surface of the ocean, becoming yet again lost in the shifting mass of my own darkness.

A knock at the door breaks my internal melancholia, and I growl to myself, sure it's Vex returning to berate me.

I rise off the bed, temper flaring at the thought of his lack of respect for me and my personal space. Storming through the water and across the room, I yank open the door, revealing not Vex, but Orion.

"Oh. It's you." I exhale, my temper extinguishing faster than an ember amid an arctic storm.

"Expecting someone else?" he asks, his royal blue fluke and the shimmering scales surrounding his eyes too bright, too fantastical for the darkness of our surroundings. He certainly doesn't belong here.

"No — I —" I begin, but he brushes past me, always one for giving a crap, sticking his nose in affairs that don't involve him.

"Oh, please, do come in, brother." I roll my eyes, slamming the door behind him and once again finding myself cocking a hip and crossing my arms over my breast scales, raising my defences.

27

"I bumped into Vex in the courtyard outside; he told me about Arabella," he expresses, frowning. I raise my hand to my head, slapping myself as I groan.

"I'm going to fucking kill him!" I vow, and Orion smiles.

"I think he kind of cares about you. It's sort of cute, actually." He gives me his mighty wisdom, and I contemplate punching him in the face. Something stops me, though; call it the *'I can't be bothered'* effect.

"You know, one of your only redeemable features that I can recall is that you hate that moron," I mutter.

"Look, we're all concerned, Azure. You're not yourself." He announces this like it's some big shocker, running his fingers through his mahogany locks, which are, as usual, effortlessly freaking tousled.

Stupid, attractive asshole.

"Really? Not myself? What about being held hostage as Queen of The Psirens sounds fun to you? I don't even want to *be* a freaking Psiren, let alone deal with the rest of them!" I exclaim. He stares at me, quizzical in his dumb expression.

"Why are you still here, then? If you hate it so much? Why don't you just leave?" He asks me this, as though I haven't tried to leave, as if the idea has never even occurred to me.

God, he's stupid.

"You remember that week where I was bedridden with a headache bad enough to make me admit I actually love you as a brother? Remember how delirious I was?" I demand, recalling how I had wanted to carve my brain out of my skull just to stop the torment, the images, the screams. That was the thing about Poseidon; he might not be visibly present, but the second I had decided I'd had enough of this place and tried to leave the city for good, the mind-numbing agony of his visions had started. The destruction the Psirens would cause without my help came to me in a three-hundred-and-sixty-degree, surround sound, three dimensional and fully immersive hell, beamed right down into my head courtesy of the gods themselves.

"What, so you're saying that happened because you tried to leave? When did you try to leave?" He looks shocked, as if he can't believe he missed my little attempt to make a break for it. As though I'd leave a neon sign or news bulletin lying around for him to find?

I'm not that kind of girl.

One day I'll just be gone.

"Yeah, it was a week after your wedding; that's how fast I was over this ridiculous attempt at democracy. I am not the right person for this job. If there is one," I reveal. He cocks an eyebrow.

"The gods don't seem to think so," he reminds me, taking a stroke forward. I back up automatically, putting more space between us as I reach the mattress and perch on the edge, bored with the conversation.

"The gods don't know their asses from their elbows. As is evidenced by the very reason we're having this stupid conversation. Poseidon screwed up by even creating the Psirens, so what makes you think that him deciding I'd make a great ruler isn't that same poor judgement?" I demand. He laughs.

"I guess you have a point there." He doesn't try to convince me I'm right for the job, which I appreciate. He at least realises, more than anyone and from personal experience, that you can't force someone into being a good leader; they must grow into and choose it in their own time.

"So, I assume you'll be heading to England?" he continues. I give him a confused stare, narrowing my eyes.

"Why would you assume that?" I ask him, and he shrugs, scratching the perfect edge of his jawline.

"Don't you want to see where she's buried — my niece?" he asks, and I feel my heart falter. He's shaming me, and I know that the only reason it's working is because I know a good mother would go, even an absent one.

I sigh out. I guess I'm not a good mother, then. The idea terrifies me more than anything I can recall.

"Arabella, her name is—" I swallow hard. "*Was* Arabella," I whisper, voice cracking as I feel my soul break. Speaking her name is always painful, but now it's even closer to home as I must accept I missed it. I missed her life.

"I think you need to go, Azure. I mean, I know I only found out about this recently, but I think it's a large part of why you're having so much trouble dealing with the Psirens."

I shrug, heart beating slowly in my chest.

"How did you leap to that conclusion?" I demand, curious more than angry at this point; I've used all my rage up on Vex, or so it would seem.

"Ruling people is a lot like being a parent. Maybe you're feeling inadequate because you feel you failed Arabella as a mother."

Wow. Where the hell did that come from?

I ponder this for a moment, pursing my lips as I feel the sting of his words.

"Do you think I failed her, then? As a mother?" I'm direct with him, and he cocks his head, brow furrowed in sadness.

"Of course not. Why would you even ask that? I think the fact you're having so much trouble deciding whether to go to her grave is enough to show you care deeply, even after all this time. It's also why you should go." He's full of wise words today. Dramatic and meaningful, no doubt, but are they true? I look at him and see much of our father in his gaze, the way his mouth is stoic in its straight and harsh line, waiting for me to decide.

"I guess I could use a break from all this madness," I concede, relief flooding my knotted gut the moment I speak the words. Orion looks relieved too, his face turning kind.

"I'll get Georgia to book you and Vex a car and a hotel, okay?" I scowl, instantly becoming tense within seconds yet again.

"Vex? I'm not having him coming along! I don't need some dirty minded tour guide for this! I've already made that very clear to him!" I exclaim, and Orion laughs.

"Azure, I'm not letting you drive a manual car again as long as I'm breathing. Remember Italy? Huh?" He's teasing me, and I scowl.

"Hey, they have THREE pedals!"

"And that's exactly why you need a guy with plenty of appendages to accompany you. Besides, you're queen now; I'm not sending you without protection." He's serious, being ridiculously over protective as usual, and I smirk.

"One of us will be needing protection, and it won't be me. I'll murder him, Orion!" As the words leave my lips, Orion smirks, and I give him a sly look.

"Are you sending me off intending to get Vex killed? Because you know that's not very ruler-ish." I fold my arms, flicking my tail up behind me, creating a flurry of frustrated bubbles as I scrutinise him.

"Not killed — just maimed. Teeny bit?" He places his fingers ever so slightly apart, showing the size of his intent, and I roll my eyes.

"Do I actually have to go with him?" I ask him, and he shakes his head with a small, smug smile.

"I think you do, actually. He knows where the grave is, and I doubt he's going to give up the location. He *really* wants to accompany you."

His expression turns suggestive, and I reach forward to slap him on the arm.

"Just shut up with that. It's never going to happen. EVER." I assure him, and he nods.

"Suuuure. Let's be honest. I just want him to screw someone else I love so I can punch him over it." Orion looks cocky, which has me shaking my head.

"Because that worked out so well for you last time," I reply with a snide tone, and he scowls, puffing out his chest. Now, it matches his ridiculously over inflated sense of pride.

"Hey, I won that fight!"

Here we go again—

"You did not! Stop being an ass. I'll think about the trip, okay?" I relinquish, and he shrugs.

"Okay, well, I'm going to go. I have to clean up the mess from today with the other council members," he says, looking awkward now. I flop back on the bed.

"Have fun with that!" I call after him as he propels himself toward the front door before opening it and slipping through.

The door slams behind him, leaving me alone with my thoughts once again.

I sigh.

When you're me, it's a terrible state to be sure.

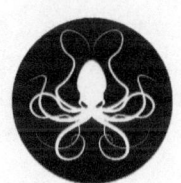

3

EYE SPY

I'M SWEPT AWAY FROM the Occulta Mirum, leaving Gideon and Callista now temporarily in charge of the mess I'm leaving behind, by a whirlpool that will take Vex and I to Scotland. From here we will journey south to some English seaside town I've never heard of.

Vex tries to make small talk as we pass from the merciless torrent of the thrashing portal and into the familiar murky green of Scottish waters, but I ignore him, finding my only source of comfort the silence that I can make us both suffer.

The water is chill, scented like fresh evergreen vegetation. It's not as cold as The Deep or The Arctic, and yet it brings a certain edge to my senses, which have been dulled by the warm embrace of the Pacific, as it flies over my skin with a refreshing icy burn. It's sharp, pungent even, as it is pulled through my gills and slips, slick, down my gullet. Perhaps the clement waters and shallow depth of the Occulta Mirum are making me soft, or maybe I'm just making excuses.

I don't know where we're going, but I know this trip isn't a vacation. I'm here to find something I've lost, or perhaps to grieve the realisation that it can never be found. Either way, I'm eager for it to be over and even more anxious to ensure that Vex doesn't ruin it for me.

We cut through the water side by side, and I let my stroke become furious against the cold tide as I find the freedom I've been so craving, even if it is only temporary. The chill of the waves gives me a mental clarity I have lost while the sun sets over-head, and I rise to the surface, exploding through the salty foam and arching my body. Vex doesn't join in but merely watches me with interest as I hit the surface of the water over and over again, hard.

After several hours he surfaces, eyes glinting rich violet under the low-hanging moon and reflecting the crisp starlight at me. He squints out to shore, satisfied as he dips back beneath the swift sway of the surface, before pulling me after him.

I yank my wrist from his grasp, not complaining but trying to substantiate that I can follow him without being manhandled.

It's weird after a while, the silence, but I don't have the inclination to break it, or the desire to make any sound at all. After all, I'm still silently seething that he's accompanying me and that he's manipulated both Callie and Orion into believing his presence is so essential.

Nearing and passing the shoreline, we propel inland, nothing beneath the surface of interest except a lot of discarded plastic and other rubbish, demonstrating the fact that humans are not worthy of this place. Perhaps Poseidon is more than aware of this grim reality; perhaps he's realised mortals need to be eliminated altogether and so tasked the worst of us with their destruction.

He tasked me.

Finally, we reach our destination.

Looking at the partiality of the moon out of habit, I close my eyes, cleaving myself from the sea. My scales fade to flesh as I phase, tickling me. Then I climb, nude, onto the wooden deck of the harbour in this sleepy seaside village. Boats bob effortlessly above the water, the air ripe with the smell of fish fresh from the day's catch, and ropes that anchor boats to wooden tethers shiver, frayed edges vibrating in the breeze.

Before us stand two men in suits, holding torches which cast a too bright light. My pupils dilate fully, exposing me as monstrous as I raise a hand to shield my eyes. Vex stands next to me, dripping.

"Azure, Vex?" they enquire in unison, and I nod, hair sodden and dripping down my torso as I move the tangled mass to cover my bare breasts.

"Yeah, well done, mate. Got any clothes? I'm getting a bloody shrivel on!" Vex complains as one of the suited men tosses a duffel bag to him.

"Get dressed. We'll take you to your vehicle when you're ready." The one who speaks has dark hair and looks unimpressed. I wonder if Callie Fischer would receive such a frosty reception. I doubt it.

I hear Vex unzip the duffel bag, but don't turn to watch him rummage through the contents, instead staring after the two men who turn from us and make their way back up the dock. It sheens beneath my feet, slick with grime and sea water as the wind rips any warmth from my skin, but still I refuse to claim whatever clothes wait for me in the bag. I have seen enough of Vex's naked body for a lifetime, with and without tentacles.

"Catch!" Vex calls and I turn, taking a step back on my bare foot as a large black towel hits me square in the chest. Wrapping it around myself, it absorbs the sea water and salt from my skin as I ring out my inky black tresses, watching goosebumps invade my flesh despite my resistance to the cold.

Vex dries himself and dresses in a black t-shirt which, might I add, is entirely too tight, some black worn jeans, and a leather jacket before completing the ensemble with steel-toed boots. After he's done, he hands me the bag and I grab a long-sleeved black turtleneck sweater, some black skin-tight jeans, and knee-high flat leather boots. I slip them on over a black lace bra and thong before pulling out one last garment. It turns out I have a similar leather jacket to Vex, but I leave it in the bag as I zip it back up, rolling my eyes.

As if this trip isn't bad enough already. Matching leather jackets? Really? What are we, like a team now? I curse, rolling up the sleeves on my sweater and leaning forward slightly so I can flip my damp hair back over my head. Water seeps through the fabric of my shirt, making my lower back cold, but I ignore it, throwing the bag over my shoulder and heading promptly after the two torch-wielding men.

As I reach the end of the wooden jetty, I gaze out into the town, taking in the scene before me. Tiny roads thread between quaint houses made of cobblestone and brick with low roofs. The buildings stand in a long line opposing the harbour, adorned with strings of multi-coloured lights that twinkle in the dark. Wreaths are nailed to doors, blackout curtains drawn, and a noticeable chill makes my breath fog in front of my face.

I guess it's almost Christmas.

"Where are we again?" I demand, scrutinising one of the men as I catch up to the identical duo.

They stand, broad backs to the water, a few inches from a low hanging stone wall, waiting with matching stoic expressions. I wonder momentarily if they're twins because if I didn't know better, I'd think I was seeing double.

"Whitby, love." The voice curls through the air like smoke and over my shoulder, reminding me that Vex, who I've stormed right past with blissful ignorance, will continue to be an irritating presence.

"I didn't ask you." I glower at him. He snorts, folding his leather-clad arms across his chest.

34

"Well, I'm telling you, anyway. That's why I'm here. Tour guide, right?" He's trying to break the tension as he lifts a hand, slicking back his silver hair, which reflects moonlight in a too bright and wet sheen. I wonder why he's even bothering; it's not like I give a crap what he looks like.

"Whatever. Where's the car?" I ask them, breathing deeply. They look suddenly uncomfortable. "What?!" I bark, watching as one of them rummages around in the inner pocket of his tight, tailored suit jacket.

"We've been given specific orders not to give you the keys. He's the driver," the man informs me, causing my eyes to narrow as I give him an exasperated stare.

"Are you freaking serious?" I voice my disdain, and he nods, expression unamused and emotionless as the breeze fails to move even a hair out of place.

"Yes. We were also told by your brother to simply say the word 'Italy', if you objected." Vex smirks as he approaches my left side with caution, masking his laugh with a cough. I whirl on the ball of my foot.

"What?! What's so funny?!" I snarl, temper rising to boiling point in an unexplainable rush.

"Nothing. Uh — well, I was just thinking about that story. Isabella told me." He coughs again, covering his mouth. I scowl.

"Look, whatever, *where's the car?*" I demand again. Vex steps forward with an outstretched hand. Taking the keys in his palm, he examines them with a furrowed brow.

"That's funny—"

He sounds confused, and I turn again.

"What? What could possibly be funny about a set of keys?" I insist, tired of his presence. He smirks before his lips twist into a look of uncertainty.

"Well, I asked Orion for a classically British car. You know, something with style. I was hoping for an Aston Martin. I used to know this girl — loved those bloody cars. She let me drive hers once. Right little spitfire she was. Red head, nice arse, thing for leather pants." He gets carried away with this internal reverie, licking his bottom lip. I growl audibly, wanting to get moving.

"Vex! Stick to the point!" I scold him, and he shakes his head, as though his vision of the redhead with a nice rear has been shattered by my high-pitched tone.

"Oh, well, these aren't really modern. They're not even battery powered. Where's the car?" he asks the two stoic individuals. They turn, pointing in silence down the road.

On the bend of the quiet street where only a few street lamps illuminate the path, a miniscule, bright yellow car sits.

"Oh, bloody hell!" Vex complains, and I exhale, my breath visible in the cold of the night.

"I am NOT getting into that thing with you!" I protest, immediately horrified at being in such tight quarters with him.

"You think I want to drive a bloody mini cooper? A *classic* mini cooper, no less? Are you nuts!? I saved the bloody world, and I get a goddamn mini? And in yellow? What about me and my badassery screams that '*beauteous butternut*' is my favourite colour to you?" He looks appalled, and I sigh, knowing I need to remember the reason we're here. It's not about Vex or how much I hate him. It's about Arabella.

"How far is it to wherever we're going?" I enquire with haste. He glances at me, seemingly nervous, as I place a hand on my hip and breathe in the crisp saltiness of the air with an exasperated glare.

"About two and a half hours," he announces. I turn to the men on my right, taking control of the situation because apparently no one else is up for the challenge.

"What's the time? Check in for the hotel ends at 11:30pm, right?" I demand, and they nod, synchronised and continually stiff in posture.

Both look at their identical watches, but only one speaks. It's interesting, as I notice only now that neither of them has a British accent.

"It's seven thirty."

"We better get going; we might be late. And I'm not sleeping out on the street," I complain, striding past them and moving through the amber glow of the streetlights. I hear Vex's tread, heavy in my wake, the hard metal of his steel-toed boots clipping the concrete, which is beginning to frost. The scent of smoke from nearby chimneys fills the air as I put space between the marina and me and inhale it fondly. Reaching the car, I find it hard not to lose my cool at the fact it's only smaller in person.

"Before I get into this lemon meringue death-trap with you, I should probably ask, where are we going exactly?" I place my arm on the roof of the car, which only comes up to my breasts at a push.

"Lincoln," is Vex's only reply as he angrily slots the keys into the door and turns them. I watch, fascinated, as he squeezes like a contortionist into the driver's seat.

Pulling open my door, I duck down and look into the interior as Vex pushes the driver's seat as far back as it'll go.

"Oh, crap," I cuss, throwing the duffle bag onto the back seat.

Vex sighs.

"Hoping it would be bigger on the inside?" He looks as if this is some kind of joke I should get, but I don't. Instead, I shrug, lowering myself into the car, which is cold and smells of stale chemical residue. My head is only a few inches from the roof, and Vex's neck is bent as he peers through the tiny windscreen.

"This is bloody cosy." He rolls his eyes, slamming his door shut and ramming the keys into the ignition. I close mine, too, not bothering to put on the seatbelt. Propping my feet up on the dash, Vex looks at me with a cocked brow.

"Comfy, love?" he smirks, and I scowl.

"My coffin had more room than this shit can," I complain. Before I can ask him what he's doing, he reaches out, putting his hand between my legs.

"Woah, what the hell do you think you're doing?" I yell, and he rolls his eyes with a snort.

"I'm trying to get to the glove compartment, love," he sighs. I drop my legs, placing both feet back on the floor as he reaches into the seamlessly hidden compartment in front of me.

Inside, the license and registration for the vehicle are stored, as well as a wallet stuffed full of cash for the three-day trip. Atop it all, something catches his attention and his eyes light up.

"Alright, now we're talking!" he exclaims, pulling out the carton of cigarettes and slamming the small compartment shut yet again. He takes out a cigarette, placing it between two fingers and raising it to his lips. Patting down his chest, he looks momentarily horrified before checking the glove compartment again. He reaches across my body as he does so, and I flinch, scowling at him.

"This is bloody Onion's doing. Piss-take of a car, fags and no light. That arsehole!" he curses out my brother, and I roll my eyes again, finding myself unable to stop.

"Can we just go, already?!" I burst, frustrated as all hell. Despite the cold of the English night outside, the temperature within this matchbox of a car is now rising quickly each second I'm stuck inside, causing increasing claustrophobia at Vex's proximity.

"Alright, alright. Keep your bloody hair on! I'm going!" he grunts, taking the cigarette from his lips and slotting it into the pocket of his leather jacket for safekeeping.

Turning the key in the ignition, the car trembles to life, the metal shell surrounding us vibrating as if it's too frail to handle the engine. "And away we go!" Vex gives a victorious smile and stares at me with far too much enthusiasm.

As we pull away from the curb, the entire car thuds to the ground, the tyres on the left side of the vehicle making sudden and unapologetic contact with the cobblestones of the road.

I don't respond to Vex's ridiculous smile, and have no desire to pass this trip in anything but silence, so I sit back and try to relax.

He spins the steering wheel back to straighten us on the road, and I look out of the tiny window, flipping the two men in suits the bird as we pass. A smirk forms, wicked, on my lips.

The stones beneath the car are making it shudder and shake with increasing ferocity as we drive over them, and I can feel every single one in the base of my spine. I tense in my seat as we turn onto a smoother road, moving not so discreetly past houses where ordinary families will soon lie dreaming.

Under the chill of the winter sky, we leave Whitby and head out in search of she who was my family, and who had stopped dreaming long ago.

Vex apparently tires of the silent treatment, and as we pull onto what he informs me is a 'dual carriageway', to absolutely no response from me, he fidgets beside me.

As we crawl down the wide road, wheels pitiful in their attempt at speed, Vex starts to hum.

I ignore him, turned toward the window and giving nothing but a blank stare to the passing blur of identical trees, quaint looking pubs with ridiculous names like *The Cock Inn*, and the odd gas station. Soon, though, he starts tapping his fingers on the leather of the steering wheel, an irritating, grating rhythm.

I don't turn. I don't want him to know he's annoying me, but slowly, despite how hard I try to make it otherwise, my rage starts to build.

Soon, his foot begins to tap every time he takes it from the clutch after changing gear, and his tongue picks up the infuriating melody as he clicks it against his teeth and the roof of his mouth. The sticky heat inside of the car, the smell of him, and the rattling of the mini's bodywork mixed with his continuing attempt at becoming an anatomical one-man band finally pushes me over the edge.

"*Vex!*" I bellow, and he jumps, the car swerving in its lane as he pulls a hard left on the steering wheel. The tyres screech as he rushes to correct our course and I reach over, smacking him round the back of the head as he does so, growling.

"What the bloody hell was that for?!" he yells. I glare at him.

"Can you not just shut the hell up? I don't need all your humming and your — your *stupid* foot tapping. For the love of all that is freaking sacred, just — stop!" I exclaim, eyes dilating. He looks completely mystified.

"I'm bored! I'd get better bloody conversation if I was driving a hearse!" he complains. My expression turn exasperated.

"What are you, *four*?" I berate him, realising quickly that Kayla is easier to entertain.

"This is a long ass drive, and these carriageways all look the damn same to me. I'm trying to stay alert!" He justifies his incessant need to irritate the hell out of me, voice ringing against the too thin bodywork of the car like clanging dustbin lids.

"Well, fine. Why don't we play that game? Will that shut you up?" I enquire, desperate for some solution that doesn't involve actually making conversation with him.

"What, eye-spy?" He gets a wicked look on his face. "Oh, love. I thought you'd never ask."

"I spy with my little eye, something beginning with S—" I sigh. Now I'm the one who's bored. It's been three hours, and although we've been driving forever, it seems like we're never going to reach our destination at this rate.

"Uh — super sexy Vexy?" Vex gestures to himself, a smirk on his lips as he pulls into a layby and turns around for the fourth time this hour.

"No. Someone who is lost!" I reveal. He rolls his eyes, predictable as ever.

"I'm not bloody lost!" he protests, and I cross my arms, scowling.

"Look, just ask for directions! You clearly *are* lost; we were supposed to be there half an hour ago and I don't even see any signs for Lincoln!" I yell. Vex pushes down hard on the accelerator, channelling his anger into something that isn't me, as we re-join the sparse, fast-moving traffic.

"I am the vessel of bloody Poseidon! The vessel of bloody Poseidon doesn't ask for bloody directions! It's fine!" he shouts in an almost growl, and I feel my expression turn shocked at his tone.

"The vessel of bloody Poseidon is *BLOODY LOST*! Ask for freaking directions, or I'm going to punch you in your fat head!" I threaten. He slouches forward over the steering wheel, peering with a furious expression through the tiny windscreen, showing no sign of slowing down.

I lurch forward, slapping his arm and hitting my head on the roof of the car at the same time as I go for him. He swats me away.

"Stop! Bloody get off me you shitting psycho!" he complains, putting one hand on my face and holding me back as I try to reach him with my arms. They're only just too short, so there is that. "Ha! There it is! Lincoln! This way!" He looks to me, eyes triumphant as we move onto a roundabout and he relinquishes control of my face.

As we whirl around the weird junction, I'm sure we've been around this stupid thing more than once tonight, and as it is, the constant motion in the motoring equivalent of a go-kart is making me feel sick.

"We better be there soon. If we miss check-in, I'm sleeping in the car and you're out on the street." I ball my fists in my lap and slump back in my seat, which squeaks beneath my weight.

"Trust me, if we get there without me killing you, I'm never getting in this damn car with you again. That's a bloody promise, love." He makes the vow and I cock my head, giving him a beyond irritated glare.

Yes, because I'm the problem here.

We fall back into furious silence as, over the horizon, a building lit up with amber flood lights from below comes into view. It's raised on a hill above the surrounding city.

"There's Lincoln cathedral," Vex informs me, and I nod, looking down at my nails and then out of the window. The land is flat, with fields stretching out into the dark on either side of us as the roads become narrower and more deeply embedded in the countryside.

When we reach the city, we pass a multitude of pubs, the names of which continue to make me laugh.

The Nosey Parker? I mean, really?

Who would name their business that?

Vex grows visibly more relaxed as we drive toward the city centre and around another enormous roundabout. We pass a fast-food restaurant, which lies opposite an architecturally abnormal site lit up with signs boasting 'University of Lincoln' as its name.

"Did you, uh — go to school here?" I ask Vex as we stop at a set of traffic lights.

"What, here? Oh, fuck no! I mean — no. I went to Oxford," he explains, and I shrug, not sure what the big deal is with the university. It looks pretty massive to me as far as schools go. Then again, my school had been my father's fishing boat, so I guess I have nothing to compare against.

The lights flash emerald and we jerk into motion as Vex drives over the bridge in front of us, turning left and making his way over a set of train tracks. A stretch of water expands out of my window, and I wonder why I've been through this hell if we could have just swum via the rivers to get here.

"Wait — they have a river that runs right through here? You mean I've been in this clown car for no reason?!" I exclaim and Vex sighs.

"Look, yes, we could have swum here. But I grew up in this town, and I've seen what students do in the Brayford Pool. You wanna climb out and find yourself covered in puke or worse? Plus, I didn't really want to watch you get into a fistfight with a swan," he explains, snappy now as both our tempers are getting frightfully short.

Well, I think, *that's ridiculous.*

Swans don't even have fists.

"Worse? What's *worse* than puke?" I demand next, ignoring the fact that his answer actually makes logical sense. He breathes out heavily.

"You don't want to know—" he mumbles as we speed around the corner, turning away from the Brayford Pool and moving deeper into the city.

He pulls the car into a parking lot, or what is signposted as a 'car park', and turns off the engine. I pocket the cash from the glove compartment, and he rises from the driver's seat and into the night air, obviously glad to be free of the car's confines and my proximity.

I'm glad. At least I know he hates my company as much as I despise his.

"Where now, oh dirtiest of tour guides?" I ask, slamming my car door shut as he locks his. I've left the duffel bag on the back seat, but I can't see myself needing the jacket. Even if I want it, I guess I can always come back for it tomorrow after sunset.

"Come on, we don't want to miss check-in." Vex turns away from the car, and I follow him past a grubby-looking hair salon and onto a pathway running parallel to the river as it ebbs through the city. When I look to the right, I see a bridge with the words, *where have you been?* carved on the side, and my brow furrows.

Why would anyone write that?

"Hey, why does that bridge want to know where I've been?" I demand, curious, and he shrugs.

"I dunno, love. It's art," he explains. I scowl, the scent of alcohol laced through with the aroma of thick crust pastry hanging heavy in the air.

"On a bridge? That's weird," I note, and he chuckles.

"You think that's weird? This little tunnel we're about to walk through is called *The Glory Hole*." I scowl yet again, wondering just how stupid he thinks I am.

"Oh, *ha, ha*. Make fun of the centuries old immortal who doesn't know things about the modern world. Aren't you a clever dick?" I bite out, but he doesn't speak. He simply gestures to a sign on the top of the oddly angled brick tunnel. It reads, *The Glory Hole*.

Well, shit.

"British people are weird," I conclude, and Vex laughs, voice echoing as we take a mere three steps before emerging on the other side of the tunnel.

"I have tentacles most of the time. I'd say British people aren't that weird," he counters. Shrugging, I speed my walking pace as we make our way up several crooked stairs and out onto what looks like a main high street.

"Come on, we've got to get to Steep Hill. The Wig and Mitre is at the top," Vex orders me, grabbing my hand, which I yet again promptly snatch back before giving him a querying look.

"Steep Hill? What is that, ironic? Like it's flat or something? Because you know there was nothing glorious about that tunnel." I voice my disappointment; I mean, with a name like that I'd been expecting more than a grubby hovel.

"No. It's absolutely not ironic. That thing is like — bloody steep," Vex informs me. I snort, unimpressed by his stamina.

"Oh, come on, it can't be *that* steep. You're just a wimp. We're immortal!" I continue to condemn him as we slip past clubs overflowing with drunks and then into a quieter street surrounded by boutiques and yet more pubs on either side. As we reach the end of the road, which is paved with more troublesome and thick cobblestone, I see Steep Hill.

Okay, so maybe it is a little steep. I muse internally, staring at the way the hill curves upward at a seventy-five-degree angle to the ground. It's bizarre because shops and tiny cottages line either side, tracing the curve, too. I wonder how anyone can live on such an incline.

"Come on then, Miss Immortal. Get a bloody move on, then." Vex pushes me forward so I don't hesitate in tackling the hill, regretting my condemnation of the name before. I grab onto the railing provided as my legs start to burn halfway up. My breath comes in short wisps, and I wonder if this is how mortals feel when they're swimming.

Is it really this difficult for them? I can scarcely remember.

I fight gravity all the way up, but eventually, I find myself at the top, completely out of breath and red in the face. Vex looks smug as he reaches the height of the hill just after me.

"Not so bad, huh?" he asks me, not even slightly out of breath.

How? He's a smoker! I wonder, pissed.

He stops beside me a moment, turning to stare at the Cathedral, which towers over and above everything else in the old-fashioned looking courtyard. A castle is at our backs, and everything here seems to be from a different time. In front of the enormous stone arch leading through to the medieval construct, I see it. The Wig and Mitre.

"Finally!" I exclaim, ready to get away from Vex and settle in with my own company. I stride forward toward the Tudor front pub, which is whitewashed on the outside and held together by rustic looking dark wooden beams. Reaching the front door, I push down on the hard wood to let myself in.

It doesn't budge.

"Hey, wait, what's the time?!" I demand, panicking. In answer to my question, and as Vex's gaze turns glazed with irritation, the bells from the Cathedral ring out. After twelve heavy and deep tolls, I realise we're far too late.

So, what now?

"This is all your fault!" I yell, turning and shoving him in the chest with both hands.

"What? How is this my bloody fault?!" he exclaims, face turning ugly and incredulous.

"You should have asked for directions!" I yell, probably waking up the surrounding residents but refusing to care.

The street lamps flicker, leaving orange flashes illuminating sharp cheekbones as I stare at Vex, fuming. He growls, grabbing my wrist and pulling me behind him.

"Stop! Where are we going?" I hiss, trying to prevent him from moving me but unable to as I realise his fist is balled in the fabric of my sleeve. He's clearly had enough of my attitude for today, of which I'm proud, as he doesn't even reply. He simply continues to march me through back alleys and tiny streets, all atop the hill that looks out over the city.

Finally, he slows, composing himself and letting me go.

"Shut up, and follow my lead, alright?" he growls. I frown, confused by his sudden anxiety. We're near where the hill descends again on the opposite side from where we've just come. Here, Vex stills in front of a tiny crooked house, of which even the miniature wrought-iron gate is slanted with the hill.

He lets himself inside and moves two paces down the delicate, quaint garden path. The smell of spearmint and honeysuckle crawls over my skin, making my stomach roll as I sight the plants growing along the sides of the house beside the front door.

"Vex!" I hiss, not content with the idea of breaking and entering. It's bad enough I'm on this trip with him; I'm so not up for sharing a jail cell with him, too.

"Shhhh!" He turns back, violet eyes flashing dangerously as his thick finger comes up to my lips. I glare at him, pissed, but do as he insists, buttoning my lip as he approaches a red front door with a slanted frame.

He looks suddenly nervous, taking a deep breath in and then exhaling as he straightens, squaring his round beefy shoulders inside his jacket.

Raising a fist, he knocks three times.

Several moments and audible rummaging later, the hall light illuminates the glass pane of the downstairs window. The door swings open with a creak several seconds after, revealing a tiny woman of only four foot eight in a robe, slippers, and flannel pyjamas.

"Chase?" she expels the single word out into the dark as I stand in Vex's shadow.

I do a double take.

Chase? Who the hell is Chase? Am I missing something? I wonder, stunned.

Vex steps over the threshold, taking the woman into his arms.

44

"Hi, Mum," he breathes.

4

MUMMY'S BOY

I STAND, AWKWARD, BEYOND the threshold where the mother and son embrace, stunned. Vex — Chase — whoever the freaking hell he actually is, mentioned he grew up here, but I hadn't expected us to make a house call and drop in on his family. I mean, how is he expecting to explain his absence? His drastic change in appearance and sudden aversion to natural sunlight?

The tungsten glow of the hall light floods the garden path, and I cast a shadow upon it as Vex steps aside, revealing me standing in the dark behind him.

"This is Azure." He introduces me, and I step forward. Placing my hands in my pockets, I attempt to avoid human contact with the woman who birthed the person who is arguably my arch nemesis.

"Hi." I'm curt with my response, caught off guard and entirely unready to make small talk, let alone pleasantries. The tiny woman looks me up and down, pulling her robe closed as I tower over her, and visibly swallows. I smile, trying to ease the atmosphere, but it's sometimes easy to forget how intimidating I can seem to mortals.

"Why don't you come in for a cup of tea? I'm sure you'd like to get in out of the cold," she suggests, stepping aside as I make my way through the door and close it behind me. The smell of spiced apple envelops me and my feet sink into the rich beige of the carpet, the homeliness of the place immediately invasive. There's a narrow staircase in dark wood pressed against the left wall of the hall, but I can't see upstairs as the landing is obscured. "Builder's tea? Earl grey, Chase?" his mother calls over her flannel covered shoulder as she pads down the warm space and into what is presumably the kitchen at the end of the hall.

Vex looks to me, his gaze not the least apologetic but slightly vulnerable as he replies, "Earl grey please," with a small cough. He looks at me, but I shake my head.

"Nothing for me — thank you," I call after her. I have no desire to drink anything at this point, let alone tea. I mean, I knew he was British, but I guess I wasn't expecting his origins to lie rooted so deeply in the unapologetically traditional English stereotype.

"Go through to the living room, love." He jerks his head, gesturing to a door on my right.

Stepping through without hesitation, I'm tired of the too bright, too warm light from the hallway and seek relief in less imposing surroundings. I mean, where's a cave when you need one?

Inside, I find a sitting room which is entirely spotless. Turning on a lamp next to a cream leather armchair, the space is illuminated, revealing a further spectrum of beiges and making the homeliness of the place seem inescapable. A wooden hearth surrounds a tiny crooked fireplace, and beside it a fat, uncouth Christmas tree stands, draped in gold tinsel, strung lights, and baubles.

I take a seat as Vex follows me, dropping to the couch opposite the fireplace and propping the heavy weight of his steel-toed boot upon his knee. He's silent as I stare around, possibly more uncomfortable than I have ever seen him, only increasing my anxiety from the banality of it all.

The atmosphere becomes excruciating as his mother joins us, carrying a tray with a teapot and china cups upon saucers, which clatter with the nervousness of her motion. She sits in an identical armchair, facing me, placing the tray on the coffee table between us. She's laid out three cups for some reason I can't discern.

"So, are you going to tell me why you're here at such a late hour, Chase? Is everything alright? You didn't mention you'd be home for Christmas." She looks concerned, and I feel my brow furrow. She's awfully relaxed about this for someone whose son has been dead to the world for almost half a year.

"Well, uh, I got sick. In the states. It's been a bit shit, actually." He coughs, hiding the fact he's lying with an extreme lack of subtlety. Reaching forward and pouring himself some boiling hot water into the fine china teacup, he proceeds to dip a tea-bag into the contents with expert precision.

"Language, Chase!" she scolds him, and I smirk. That's the least of her worries where he's concerned.

"Sorry, mum. Uh, anyway, we caught this rare sensitivity to the sun. That's why we're here. We need a place to crash. Please." He implores her with wide and momentarily childlike eyes, and my gaze travels to the walls and mantelpiece. Pictures of him as a baby, naked on a faux fur rug with a cheeky grin, and then as a small child riding his bike, line the walls in a kind of morbidly fascinating chronology that leaves me staring. My eyes finally fall on a picture of him in a graduate's cap and gown which sits, tilted to face me, on the mantel. Examining the photograph, which stands next to his framed BA in English Literature, I realise that he really hasn't changed that much at all.

"Do you have this sickness, too?" She gazes at me, curiosity laced through the warm depths of her brown irises, and I nod, not speaking the lie. Drumming my long fingernails against the armrests of the chair, my breathing becomes stilted, forced even, under the anxiety of his mother's gaze.

"Well, I had better get on the phone to that university first thing in the morning! How could they not tell me? You could have died!" she exclaims, voice becoming high pitched and grating. Vex leans forward, taking a sip of his tea and frantically swallowing — probably burning his tongue in the process — as he rushes to speak.

"Ma! It's fine. It's not the university's fault. I'm twenty-two; it's my fault. I know I should have called you sooner, but it's been a big adjustment. It's something in the water, and it only affects a few people per million. You shouldn't worry so much. Really. It's fine. We're fine," he protests, frantic in trying to hide the unimaginable truth. His mother cocks an eyebrow, her unkempt hair almost vibrating around her ears. I continue to watch the spectacle between them with outside interest.

She looks furious as she moves to make her own tea, as though in practicing this very British art, her problems and worries will magically disappear. Vex leans back as she eyes him wearily, and I finally feel the need to speak.

"I think they're running an investigation, actually. I'm sure it's being taken care of. That'll teach Chase here to go swimming in unknown waters, though, won't it?" I smile at him, eyes glinting wickedly as he narrows his gaze at me. Raising his cup to his lips once more, he fails to make an adequate comeback.

"Well, it is late. Of course, you can stay. Is there anything you need?" his mother enquires. I shift in my seat, wondering if I can ask her to teach her son not to be an asshole at this late stage.

"Blackout curtains. Do we have those old ones from grandma's place?" he asks her. She nods.

"Of course. I'll go fish them out now." She looks calm again, in her element, as she exits the room with swift grace and abandons her tea. It continues to steam visibly as the scent of bergamot fills the room with an unrelenting ferocity, becoming even more overwhelming as it mixes with the seasonal spiced apple. My gaze falls on Vex, trying to ignore it.

"She seems — nice," I observe, trying not to be an asshole. I know that family can be a touchy subject, and I guess it's this or the yellow mini for sleeping arrangements.

"She's the bloody best. Really. Best Mum in the world." He looks after her fondly and something within me shifts, grating against my better judgement. It's like my heart has inflated temporarily, though I couldn't tell you why.

"You should head up to my room. I need to speak with her alone for a few minutes. It's a lot to take in, I guess," he explains.

Getting to my feet, I don't care where I go as long as I don't have to drink any of the vile smelling tea penetrating my nostrils full force. I swear, you could bottle it as a weapon.

"You're a good liar, at least to the mortal eye," I comment, pushing my hair behind my ear, wondering if he lies so smoothly to me and how often. He smirks, eyes hiding cocky amusement.

"It was a long, *quiet* drive. I had time to think of an alibi, just in case," he insists. I frown, shifting atop the thick padding of the carpet, somewhat uncomfortable as I hear his mother bumbling around in the hall.

"And if she finds out the truth?" I ask him, and he gives me a stern look of warning.

"I'd die before I let that happen. She's been through enough." His words catch me off guard, and I exhale heavily, feeling the tension leave my body. "Upstairs, second door on the left," he calls after me as I pass and step towards the hall.

I glimpse his mother rummaging in the cupboard under the stairs, presumably for the blackout curtains, as I stride through the doorway. I don't speak, or smile, but merely climb the stairs toward the shadow of the landing.

As I am looking to the door Vex instructed me to find, a voice calls out from behind me where another door lies open. I assumed it was the bathroom.

"Who the hell are you, beautiful?" I spin on my heel, eyes dilating to black as my Psiren instincts catch me off guard. I come face to face with a pimple faced teenage boy. He's standing in a black ripped t-shirt and boxer shorts, his figure scrawny. I scowl.

"Your worst nightmare, pipsqueak," I growl through gritted teeth, but the boy doesn't flinch. He merely crosses his arms over the profanity scrawled across his shirt and stares at me, expression dead.

"Is my brother home?" he demands. I let my body go limp, trying to calm my raging instincts.

"How should I know?" I ask, smirking as the sulky faced teen rolls his eyes and runs his hand back through his greasy black hair.

"Whatever," he replies with a grunt, pushing past me and making his way down the stairs. I pause to listen, the sounds of the two brothers reuniting easily audible through the thin floors and walls of the old house in a muffle of masculine greeting.

Striding across the landing carpet with cat-like softness, I push on the door to Chase's bedroom. I would say Vex, but the creature he's become certainly wouldn't be seen dead with the baby blue walls, posters of so-called wonder woman, and the shark plushie at the end of the bed. Or at least I don't think he would. Then again, how well do I really know him?

Not at all. Clearly. As is evidenced when I turn on the light and pace around the room. He has books, stacks upon stacks of books. I don't recognise most of the titles but finger the spines, finding myself more interested than I want to admit. His window looks out over the lopsided street outside, and I ponder how a house on a hill can be not the least bit tilted on the inside.

As I'm inspecting some comic books on the desk by the far left wall, picking up and smelling cologne bottles, and rummaging through his drawers without permission, I hear him and his mother talking, their voices floating up the stairs.

"Has he been back?" Vex asks, sentiment slightly muffled. I take a few steps toward the door, creeping for no discernible reason.

"No, he's gone. Don't worry so much. He'll never hurt me again. You know that's why we moved." His mother's strained and yet unmistakably soft and comforting tone reaches me as my heart falters in its beat. I don't really know her, but I can tell she's a great mother, a good person, more than I ever could be. The thought of someone hurting her makes me feel physically ill, something completely out of the blue and abstract for someone like me.

I stand in the bedroom, stone still, as I take a deep breath, unwillingly inhaling the scent surrounding me with unwanted fondness. This place — it's a proper home. With walls, a kitchen, tea and a hearth. It's the kind of place where happy memories can take root and flower. Silly, I know, but in the beige domesticity of this place, I find myself jealous and longing for something similar to call my own, even though I know it can never be.

Vex's footsteps sound on approach, the stairs creaking beneath his weight. I remain standing in the centre of the room, feeling like nothing more than a spare part, unwilling to make herself at home.

"You alright? Tristan didn't give you any shit, did he?" Vex asks, eyes widening with actual concern as he slips inside the room. I smirk.

"Nah. Besides, I can handle myself against a scrawny teenager."

"I should bloody hope so. Little shit. He's trying to make me feel like a fuck up for being away for so long. He has no bloody idea." He says this like we're friends, like we actually care about the stuff that happens in each other's lives.

"Yeah, well, he's a teenager. Since when do they know anything, right?" I ask him, allowing my confrontational urges to fizzle beneath the surface. The dynamic between Vex and me has changed since I stepped into his family home, and I wonder what it is about being enveloped in someone's nostalgia that does this to me.

"You alright to take the floor?" Vex asks, throwing me a blanket from the top of the stack of fabric in his arms.

"Yeah. I prefer to sleep on something hard, anyway." I relinquish this information and Vex's eyes caress me with surprise as the beginning of a dirty comeback flickers behind his pupils.

"Why's that then, love? I thought you'd pout and demand the bed," he jokes.

"I prefer not to sleep too heavily, dreams and all."

Why did I just tell him that? I wonder. The rage, which had been burning so deep in my soul for him just an hour ago, dissipates like cold spray off the sea at the height of summer.

"I've had those. Well, weird dreams, anyway. Ever since that night with Poseidon," he admits. I tilt my head at him, sitting down in the chair at his desk as he goes to hang the new pair of curtains across the narrow window. I don't reply, and as he hooks the thick fabric over the curtain rod, he gazes back at me with hooded lids.

"Of course, we don't have to sleep at all. I'm sure there are many ways to pass the daylight hours." His gaze becomes salacious, a flicker of that arrogant prick that I know him to be remaining despite the return to his origins.

"Vex. Shut up," I sigh, mentally drained from the journey. I don't really want to sleep at all, but the thought of making more small talk with him for twelve hours is just plain intolerable, so I guess I'll have to settle for the shitty, guilt-ridden dreams.

"I meant reading. Don't flatter yourself, love." He finishes putting up the drapes and then moves over to the bookshelves, which rise in dark wood from floor to ceiling. He runs his fingers along the spines as I had done only moments before and then pulls out a hefty looking leather-bound edition. I glance at the cover.

"The Bible? What? You going to try and save my soul?" I give him a deadpan expression as he opens the book and shows me the interior.

Where the pages had once been whole, he's carved out nearly the entire middle section, leaving only the margins of each page intact. In the gap he's created, a small bottle of tequila, a packet of cigarettes, and a lighter sit, hidden from prying eyes.

"Crafty." I snort at the schoolboy trick.

He empties the contents of the book and offers me the bottle, but I shake my head. "No, I don't drink," I reply, and this time it's his turn to roll his eyes.

"Priss. Shame you're not in one of those little catholic school girl uniforms with that kind of resolve." He winks at me, as if my sobriety is turning him on.

Unscrewing the lid, he moves to sit on the windowsill, observing me as he takes a swig before placing a cigarette in his mouth and lighting it with an audible click from the solid steel lighter in his palm.

"Do you have to make everything dirty?" I ask him, and he shakes his head, opening the window beside him a crack.

"No, love, it's a choice. Though, sometimes, non-sexual behaviour can be the most erotic of all—" he explains.

I frown.

"What the hell is that supposed to mean?" I demand. He puffs on his cigarette, exhaling out of the window before jumping down onto the floor and moving back over to the bookshelf. He takes off his leather jacket, slinging it over the desk chair as he bends down and selects another book before pulling it free and throwing it at me. I look down at the cover as it lands in my lap with a dull thud, the impact dislodging dust from its jacket.

"Pride and Prejudice?" I read the title aloud, and he nods, inhaling the scent of the smoke deeply as he returns to the window, exhaling the fumes out into the frosty night air.

"Yes, one of my favourite and least favourite books all in one," he informs me, putting his foot up on the sill and letting the other one dangle against the radiator beneath.

"Because?" I enquire, flicking through the pages.

I'm surprised. The print is small, and the language is eloquent. Who knew Vex was literate? He certainly doesn't act like it.

"Because Mr. Darcy is arguably one of the biggest assholes and still one of the most desirable men in English literature. He's a complete dick, and yet — hot as balls for absolutely no reason. It's where I got my name, you know," he announces, proud. I feel my eyebrow cock with unbidden curiosity.

"Chase?" I smirk, feeling the way it rolls off my tongue as wrong. The name really doesn't suit him. It's far too refined.

"No. Vexus. Mrs. Bennet, the heroine's mother, is constantly saying how vexed she is by Mr. Darcy and his terrible reputation. I wanted to be that guy."

I laugh, a genuine smile crossing my lips.

"So, you wanted to be the guy that pisses everyone off? Well, you can put a big tick in that box. You have definitely not failed," I insist, and he puckers his lips.

"Oh, you love it, though. I see you, the way you get all hot and tingly when I-" he begins, but I cut him off, crossing my arms across my chest.

"Vex me?"

"Exactly."

"I think you're deluded. Maybe all the drinking has melted your brain. I think you're an asshole," I remind him, grabbing a pillow from the end of his mattress and creating a make-shift bed on the soft padding of the navy carpet. As I lie down, I get a sniff of the smoke blowing back into the room. It makes my skin rise in goosebumps, which I promptly ignore.

"But I'm *your* asshole," Vex persists, and I roll my eyes yet again, exasperated by him as usual.

"Okay, conversation over." I put a stop to his crap right here, right now.

"Hey, you know what's nice?" I ask him, changing the subject as I put both my palms underneath my head, staring at the sloping ceiling of the room.

"What?" He sounds bored at the conversation changing, but I push on, undeterred.

"The fact I haven't had a vision since this trip started," I relinquish, and he nods, raising the glass bottle to me and then to his lips.

"Cheers to that. It's almost as if the gods and goddesses don't give a shit about our little trip into your past," he exclaims. I laugh, the sound echoing out of me in cold, unfeeling reverberations.

"That would be because they don't," I bite out, my continual sniggering becoming ever more bitter on my tongue.

"They're not as bad as you think. I had one in my head, you know." He defends them, and I snort, wondering when he got so stupid.

"You were essentially used as a human dummy for Poseidon. That doesn't make you special, you know; that makes you his little play thing here on earth." I inform him of the facts, and he sighs, snorts, and then exhales heavily before taking a relaxed puff of his cigarette as he leans back against the frosted windowpane.

"I guess it does." He doesn't argue with me but continues to smoke and drink as we let silence fall over us.

I think about his mother and realise that I have the wicked urge to make him uncomfortable.

"Who are you so scared will find your mother?" I demand, prying even though I know I probably shouldn't. Do I care about the answer? Perhaps.

"My dad," he replies curtly.

I do a double take.

"Wait, your mother is afraid of your father?" I'm surprised.

"Yeah, he used to beat the shit out of her. Until I was old enough to get in the way. Then, I used to take his rage instead. In a way, I sort of wish he'd show his face. I'd love to take him on as a Psiren. I'd bloody massacre him." He gets a dreamy look on his face, and I smile. If I were in his shoes, I'd do exactly the same thing.

"Well, if you need any help with that, you know where I am." I offer my services, the one thing I know I'm apt at, and he smiles.

"Thanks, but I think I can handle one asshole alone." He balls his fist visibly, and I can tell it deeply affects him. I don't reply again, taking in the information.

Leaning over from the window, he picks up *Pride and Prejudice* from atop the silver duvet where I left it and opens the cover. He begins flipping through the pages as he lights up another cigarette, and I watch him with half interest. Suddenly he speaks.

"Angry people are not always wise."

"Excuse me?" I exclaim, confused.

"It's my favourite quote from this book. The truest if you ask me, love." He continues to flip through the pages as I ponder this.

"Do you think that's why the Psirens are untameable? Too much rage, not even a speck of wisdom?" I ask him, and he shakes his head.

"I think you need to be the wisdom for all of us." His reply makes me shudder at my core, and I pull the blanket around myself as I turn onto my side.

"I don't have any wisdom left to give, and even if I did, nobody would care enough to listen," I mutter, irritated that he's brought it up.

"You have to *make* them listen. Especially the council. That's why Poseidon chose you. Because you're fierce enough to make them hear you above their own afflictions." Vex's voice breaks, like what he's saying is an inner truth he's been concealing for longer than any of us have known.

"And what would these afflictions be exactly?" I query him, genuinely interested despite myself. He smirks as he finishes his cigarette, flicking it out of the window before drawing the curtains and casting the room in uninterrupted black.

"The affliction of all of those put in positions of superiority, love. Pride and prejudice."

I don't know what to say to this, so I say nothing. Instead, I choose to sleep away the day. After all, it's better than listening to the advice of someone much more irritating than I— but also, apparently, wiser and surprisingly more well-read than I will ever be.

5

A GRAVE BUSINESS

HE TREMBLES, NAKED AND *tied to a simple wooden chair.*

Taking several strides forward, my tongue slips between my lips, lapping up the salt of his sweat and blood-soaked skin as I caress the side of his face with my mouth.

I feel desire pool in my stomach as I raise my pearl strung whip, leaping back onto the balls of my feet and lashing the side of his neck with an expert command of my favourite weapon. My heart is pounding in my chest, blood rushing around my metallically powerful muscles. Dilating with dark power, my eyes take in the victim of my violence as his head hangs down low, and the last cry of his agony fades to nothing against the rusted iron of the warehouse walls.

"Why are you doing this?" he whimpers, looking up at me as his damp, dark fringe falls over the desperate fatigue of his limpid green eyes.

"Why? Does there have to be a reason?" My voice is real, cold, honest. The truth is, I've been bored for days now. Titus has been busy trying to obtain the Trident of Poseidon, for a reason that is hard to discern as separate from his vanity and pride, and I have become restless. The shadow stirs within my mind, shifting like a tide readying to tumult with the power of a storm that's been brewing since long before dawn.

I tighten my grip around the hilt of my whip, excitement clutching at me before I lash out at him again. This man has done nothing wrong. Not really.

I'd picked him up in a bar, lured him back to an empty warehouse with the promise of sex, and now he will suffer for assuming I could ever even come close to being used for his pleasure.

"Aghh!" he cries out, and my lips pull back over my teeth in a feral smile. This is the first spark of joy to penetrate my armoured hide in as many days—

I startle awake, disturbed not only by the guilty hammering of my own heart, but also by the stark, white light cast down upon me. Vex has opened his laptop on the desk where he's now sitting, towering over me as I stir, too hot beneath the blanket.

"Evening, love," he calls back over his shoulder as his fingers tap audibly on plastic keys.

"What time is it?" I murmur, and he looks back over his shoulder at me momentarily before spinning the desk chair to face me.

"A little after four in the afternoon. It's now getting dark. Good dream?" he insists. I scowl.

"Not really." I sit up, avoiding eye contact with him as the familiar guilt of such a dream falls over me. Most people would think that it was the act of torturing someone that continues to leave me guilty, yet it isn't. It's the fact that I desire to do it all over again. I don't regret it. Not even close. I'm aroused by the mere prospect of reliving it, of giving into those urges which I know are forbidden. I know, though, that I must restrain these desires, wrangle them in a stranglehold, even if it breaks me.

"Could've fooled me. You were moaning something bloody fantastic." He winks, and I rub my eyes to avoid holding his gaze.

"What are you doing?" I demand, changing the subject. Sitting up with fluid motion, I push myself up onto my feet, stretching. He licks his bottom lip, eyes tracing where my shirt pulls up, exposing my bare midriff.

"I'm seeing if I can get a hold of some of the death records for Lincoln from the sixteen hundreds. Might make tonight's search a little easier," he explains. I peer over his shoulder into the stark light of the screen.

"I thought you knew where the grave was?" I exclaim. He looks at me like I'm insane.

"I know it's in Lincoln. I don't know exactly where," he admits, tearing his gaze away from my stomach too slowly as I slap him on the arm.

"You asshole! Why did you even come here with me? I could've found Lincoln on a map!" I exclaim, and he shrugs.

"I was worried about you, Azure," he admits, calling me by my name, not 'love' or 'pet' or anything else from the ridiculous dictionary of slang he thinks makes him sound cool. I look at him as we linger in this moment of gradual peace, tired of the constant battle between us.

"What's Google?" I ask, distracting him as my gaze shifts to the image behind him, and I take in the screen he's browsing. He laughs at my lack of know-how.

"It's like a search engine," he explains, and I frown. I don't get it.

"Whatever. Did you find her?" I ask.

"If I knew her last name, that would help." He stares at me, eyes wide, as though he's pitying me and the pain of my past. I debate slapping him but quell the twitch before it reaches my palm and reply instead.

"Dragos, her last name is Dragos. She was born in 1591," I inform him. He looks surprised.

"Damn. You're looking good for a FILF," he smirks, turning back to the screen and typing in a few words before slamming down on the oblong key at the bottom of his keyboard.

"FILF?" I demand, wondering why he suddenly seems to be speaking a foreign language.

"Uh, Fossil I'd like to —" I cut him off.

"Oh, fuck you!" I cross my arms, scowling at him. Why the hell did I have to get stuck with his sorry ass for this trip? He's so goddamn filthy.

"You bloody asked!" he protests, and I snort. I don't reply, but after a few minutes, Vex curses. "Damnit! Bloody arseholes!"

I breathe deep, running tentative fingers through my silken hair.

"What now?"

"Well, they're locked to the public. The bishop's records aren't available," he explains.

I shrug.

"So?"

"So, it means we have to find the bloody bishop and get him to take us to the original copies of the records. I wouldn't even know where to start looking. They could be anywhere," he explains, and my heart becomes heavy with the fear that this trip will have been for nothing. Sitting back down on his bed, I feel my frustration mounting, so grab the plush shark from beside me and throw it at Vex's head.

"Hey, watch it! No throwing Mr. Teeth!" he scolds me. I cock an eyebrow, amused.

"Mr. Teeth?"

"You try naming a bloody shark at three years old. It's hard, okay?!" He's defensive, snapping, so I raise my hands in surrender.

"Alright, Jesus! Sorry, Mr. Teeth is a very respectable name for a shark." I say this, unsure of the reaction he wants from me. He nods, smiling, clearly satisfied.

"Why, thank you, love." His mouth twists into a crooked and dangerous smile as his eyes glint. I, once again, try to stay on topic.

"How exactly are we going to find this bishop?" I vocalise the absurdity of this as a plan. We only have one night.

"Well, I think the bishop actually lives next to the Cathedral. What say you and I pay him a little house call?" he suggests. I nod, not willing to waste any more time. Vex places Mr. Teeth down gently on the bed beside me as we both get to our feet. He slams his laptop shut, the last light of day fading fast outside the window.

"Let's go."

After a rushed and teary-eyed departure from Vex's childhood home, filled with what I'm sure are entirely empty promises he will *call real soon* and *be home before you know it*, we take to the streets of Lincoln once again.

The air is fresh and cold as we walk through the high, rounded, medieval arch and into the courtyard of the Cathedral. The night is sharp with frost and everywhere people hurry through the spice infused air leaking from local pubs, making their way from one wreath-clad doorway to another.

I look up at the intimidating height of the Cathedral, wondering why they build them so tall. Could it be the more massive the building, the greater the fear of god instilled into the hearts of mortals desperate for his love? Or are the priests just incredibly insecure? The enormous spires penetrate the clear dark of the night sky, surrounded by stars, and I sigh, feeling the magnitude of the task ahead. One grave of hundreds, perhaps thousands, and I have one night to find it.

"This way," Vex instructs, leather jacket flaring out behind him as the wind picks up, moving my hair back from my face.

We pace around the semi-circular lawn outside the large double doors and toward a small house made entirely of cobblestone standing behind a high, thick-set wall. Vex pushes open a tall wrought-iron gate, and my steps become more and more defined against the cobbles underfoot as I move beneath his arm and through, wondering. What are we going to do? Sit down and have tea with the guy? I mean, I guess that seems like a very British way to handle this.

"Follow my lead," Vex instructs, and I scowl. I'm not used to taking a backseat, and yet today I wonder if I can be bothered fighting him for the position of leader.

"Why? What exactly are you intending to do?" I enquire, getting an instinctual sense he's about to try something very stupid. He shrugs.

"What I have to. I haven't come all this bloody way for nothing. We're finding the grave." He sounds determined, and suddenly I realise that he really cares about all this.

But why?

I open my mouth to ask him, but before I can, we're standing outside a wooden front door. I expect him to raise a hand, to knock, but instead he puts a hand across my chest and pushes me behind him. Bending his leg at the knee, he kicks the door in. I jump at the sudden action.

What the fuck is he doing? This so isn't tea! I cuss, watching as he bursts into the living room. It lies just behind the empty doorway, letting the cold from the outside tumble, unwanted, into the room along with his clumsy gait.

"Excuse me? What is the meaning of this?" I hear a shocked voice and then take a few steps inside the building as Vex storms across the vile mouldy green of the bishop's living room carpet. I twist, slamming the door shut behind me as Vex grabs the unsuspecting man.

Burying his fists in the man's red knit sweater, he lifts him from his armchair.

A bible drops to the floor, though as the cover opens, I see this one has actual verse in, not tequila and smokes.

"We have questions, mate!" Vex gets right up in his face, and I feel nothing. It's not the same; it hasn't been the same since the night of the blood moon all those weeks ago. This doesn't stimulate me; it doesn't arouse me. It merely bores me, as if the person I had been is completely unattainable because of my own imperative restraint. I lean against the wall, cocking my hip and watching Vex as he turns to me.

"Don't you want to rough him up a bit, love?" he asks, surprise raising the pitch of his usually deep voice. I shake my head, long dark hair brushing against my ears.

"I'm good," I respond, looking down at my nails as I swallow hard.

"Bloody great — and I thought watching you walk away from that Psiren brawl was depressing." He drops his victim down into the depths of the chair again, a small cloud of dust expelling on impact, and keeps his hand firmly on the man's shoulder as he turns to me.

60

"I've been doing this longer than you. Beating the crap out of holy men has long since lost its appeal." I make the excuse, knowing it's not true but unable to find the energy to care enough to explain.

"Bollocks! I saw you in that battle. You were like some kind of machine, the way you handled Solustus. What the hell is up with you?" he demands, face incredulous, angry almost, as the fireplace at the back of the room casts deep shadows upon his face. I shrug again.

"If I punch him, will you shut up?" I sigh, wondering what must be going through the head of the bishop. He sits beneath Vex's heavy palm, terrified yet confused as he looks between us while we bicker.

"No. Because you'll just be doing it for me. Don't you just — *crave* it anymore?" he asks me, his eyes flickering with a passion I've seen lost.

"Nope."

It's a lie. A blatant lie. But one I must tell regardless, because the person I truly am isn't a ruler, isn't respectable, isn't even half decent. She's a monster who loves being a monster, and that is no longer permissible for both the sake of my survival and the satiation of Poseidon's desire. I've long since curbed the urge, even if it has turned me empty and numb.

Vex's slashed eyebrow cocks, and I wonder what he's thinking. Giving me a final worried glance, he turns his attention back to the bishop.

"Right, mate. You're going to help us, got that?" he barks, and the bishop looks like he might say something. He begins to stand up out of the chair, but Vex takes his palm off the man's shoulder and uses it to shove him back into its hold so the entire thing rocks, unsteady on its hind legs. As I watch, his eyes dilate to black, and the bishop's face turns from determined to horrified.

"Oh, Father—" The bishop begins to pray, and I laugh under my breath. Vex puts his boot up between the legs of the man, causing the chair to slam back down onto the floor as the fire in the hearth behind him extinguishes.

"Now, now. None of that, mate. He won't help you. Only you can do that. We need to get into the death records for this place — you know, the bishop's transcripts, ones for way back when, like the sixteen-hundreds?" He gets up close to him, his face ghostly in only moonlight as his lips pull back and he smiles, eyes still abyssal, now sparking through with lilac lightning.

"Death records?" The holy man stutters, face drained of colour, and Vex nods. The bishop pushes his glasses up his crooked nose with a shaking hand.

"Yes, mate, very good. Where do I find em?" he demands, voice expectant, and the priest swallows hard. I shift from foot to foot as Vex cocks his head with impatience, wishing he'd hurry and get to the point.

"They've, uh, recently been moved. For reapplying of preserving agents to the paper." He can barely get his words out, and I take this moment to step in, sick of all this playing around. Striding around the small coffee table beside his armchair, upon which a cup and saucer steam only slightly in pitiful lukewarmth, I let my own pupils fully dilate. Pulling my lips back over my teeth just as Vex had done, I maintain as much control as I can manage.

"Where?!" I demand, and he tears his gaze away from Vex, eyes landing on me and widening. He raises a hand, moving it to his neck, but I grab it from the air.

"No crucifixes. Where are the transcripts?" I exert pressure on his wrist, threatening to crush tendons and stop the blood flow to the limb. My heart rate picks up a little, and I take a few deep breaths, curbing my excitement, knowing it's wrong. Vex looks at me, scrutinizing me, his gaze only moving from me as the bishop's voice hits the air between us.

"The Wren library," he speaks, clearly this time. I continue to grill him.

"Right, where is that?" I persist in exerting pressure, and Vex looks to me as they both answer in unison.

"The Cathedral."

"You — you —" the bishop stutters.

"What? Spit it out!" Vex exclaims. The man sighs, as if he can't believe he's speaking with us at all.

"You need a key," he explains, and Vex inhales deeply before a smirk twists his pointed features.

"I guess you're coming with us then — mate."

"My name is Christopher Lowson."

Vex's expression turns surprised.

"And I care because?" he asks, leaning back and letting the man up out of the chair.

"Don't you want to know the name of the man you're threatening?" Christopher's voice is steadier as he gets to his feet, picking up the bible from where it has fallen on the floor. Vex takes it from him quickly, flicking through the pages before throwing it behind him. I watch as the book falls into the fireplace where it smoulders among the sooty remains of tonight's dead fire.

"You won't be needing that; I assure you," Vex snarls. The bishop straightens.

"There is no mortal soul which cannot be saved, young man. No matter how far you may appear to have fallen." He speaks with ignorant certainty and Vex chuckles to himself, looking at me and placing his hand around the back of the bishop's neck.

"Who said we were mortal, mate?" he asks, and I smile as he winks at me, having the fun I'm stopping myself from indulging.

He's right though. There is no salvation here, only the power of self-restraint, the power of my will and his.

The walk across the courtyard toward the Cathedral is brisk and strained as Vex and I trap the bishop on either side. We approach the enormity of the building's doors, the lush grass on either side of us bristling noticeably in the December chill. I let the cold wrap around me like an old friend, giving me that same edge to my senses as it had when we'd first arrived.

The bishop pushes in on the doors, which creak loudly. As the echoes of the wood scraping against the cold stone of the floor fade, I hear Vex whisper.

"No funny business, or I rip you apart like a sodding Christmas cracker. Got it?" I ignore him, trying not to let myself feel either the excitement at the fact I'm once again involved in threatening someone, or nerves about the fact my daughter's grave, after everything, may remain lost to me.

I'm distracted momentarily as the hallway we're striding through widens, and the main part of the Cathedral is revealed to us in all its over pompous glory. The ceilings must be at least one hundred feet tall, if not more. The room is constructed of stone with enormous archways supporting the ceiling and bridged with golden, gilded beams from both the left and right.

Every step I take echoes, and the temperature drops even further as I stare into the length of the place, lit by only a few dim orange lights embedded into the concrete floor. The shadows of the ceiling, of the archways, and those cast over us by the back of the pipe organ standing with its back to the front doors make the medieval architecture seem cruel and unforgiving. Totally fitting when you think about it.

"Which way?" Vex barks, voice echoing carelessly as we realise that nobody is here. I have no idea what the time is, but it's only early evening, so I wonder why there aren't more people, or at least some choir boys at practice.

The priest strides with panicked efficiency, the leather of his too comfortable looking loafers making barely a sound as we scurry down the length of the hall. We continue forward as a threesome, both holding the man's arms now as if the closer we get to our destination, the more we fear we may have to subdue him. He visibly relaxes the further into the building we venture, as if he thinks God will protect him or something similarly naïve and human. If only he knew the gods; if only he knew how they love to watch us squirm underneath their invisible magnifying glasses as they burn us with their hot and unpredictable scorn. Would he love them so much then? Would he worship just the same?

I doubt it.

Making a left, we move into an offshoot of the main building. It has a low ceiling and glassless window arches revealing a small grassy courtyard outside, and is surrounded by identical looking corridors. Reaching the end point of the hall, we turn right as the bishop slides his hand into his pocket and withdraws a key, slipping it into the lock and twisting the handle. The door gives a recognisable yet squeaky click, signalling it as open.

"He couldn't have just given us the key—" I sigh, wondering why we walked him all the way here if he had the key in his pocket all along.

"I wouldn't have left him, anyway; don't need him getting the police, do we, love?" Vex reminds me, posing the question. I ponder it as we step through the door together, becoming blanketed by the darkness inside.

I guess when I'd done things like this before, I never worried about the police. That was mainly because no man lived long enough once I had gotten what I needed to be a snitch. It was an easier method to be sure, and I'm frustrated at how doing things like this, without bloodshed, can be so much more time consuming. I miss the simple life, the one of no guilt and no regret, of death and of easy, definitive conclusions to complicated problems.

Shutting the door behind us, Vex releases the man, who quickly turns on the light, illuminating our surroundings.

The bishop leads us forward, crossing the length of the room as we close in at his back. We ascend a beautiful looking spiral staircase that could have been carved from a single piece of wood and then turn as we reach the last step. The bishop unlocks yet another door with the same key he had used on the first.

Pushing them inward, we step through and yet another light switch is flicked, revealing a library with a dark wooden floor and a single wall stacked floor to ceiling with leather-bound books. Many of them may well be older than I am. The opposing side of the library houses only windows and a few chairs, and a long mahogany table stands central to the space, stacked high with boxes. Looking at Christopher, I fold my arms, impatient even still.

"Well? Where are these the record things?" I bark, and he takes a few steps over to the table.

"They're in these boxes. They're here to keep the paper preserved. We coat the pages in a—" He's getting off topic, so I interrupt him.

"Yeah, I don't really care. I just want to find someone." I brush past him, moving to take a seat at the table. Vex moves to do the same, and Christopher backs himself into the corner.

"Hey, you're not going anywhere, mate. Sit." Vex orders his compliance, pointing to the chair beside him. The bishop looks back at the door, and I cock an eyebrow.

"He would have you on the floor before you reached the door, you know," I inform him, so he exhales heavily, grabbing the cross he's pulled from beneath the V-neck of his sweater and twiddling it between his forefinger and thumb. Plopping down in the seat beside Vex, he stares at me with curiosity, and I ignore him. Vex and I each pull a box toward us and begin pulling out clusters of papers and old looking books.

It's going to be a long night.

Two hours later and the fighting has commenced. I should have seen this coming, and as the bishop sits, watching Vex and me with a half-amused gaze, I wonder why I didn't.

"Look, anything you can remember?! Anything?! My eyes are going sodding square!" Vex complains, now sitting on the floor surrounded by mountains of crinkled, aged paper.

"I told you, I gave birth to her and then bled to death. My husband freaking stole her from me! That's all I got!" I exclaim, sick of repeating the story to him. It had been bad enough reliving it when telling it to him the first time.

"Well then, in that case, we're bloody screwed. Who knew so many pissing people died in the space of a hundred years?" He throws the papers scattered around himself into the air and Christopher visibly flinches in his seat. Vex pulls out a cigarette after a few minutes as I stare at him, annoyed, and Christopher coughs slightly.

"Please — don't smoke around the books—" He implores Vex with his gaze.

"Oh, sod off, mate! You try being on this bloody field trip with little miss sunshine over there! You'll be begging me for a light." He inhales sharply, almost choking as he takes in his first lungful of smoke before exhaling and puffing a cloud of the stuff out into the room. I glare at him.

"I didn't want you to come!" I exclaim, slamming my fists down on the table.

"Well, it's a bloody good job I did come, though, isn't it? Because you'd probably have died trying to drive that yellow tin can your brother calls a suitable ride. Not to mention that if it weren't for me, you wouldn't have known we even needed to find the bloody bishop's transcripts!" He inhales again after his rant, the tip of the cigarette glowing visibly as he slams his head into the bookcase behind him in an overly dramatic plight.

"I'd have figured it out! I don't need you! I can find my goddamn daughter's grave on my own!" I exclaim.

The bishop's eyes suddenly turn wide.

"Your daughter? But — why are you looking so far back?" he asks, glaring at me like I'm insane as I turn to him.

"It's none of your goddamn business!" I yell. He cocks his head.

"Look, I should probably be furious at you two, but you really don't seem to know what you're doing, and I don't really want to be sitting here all night. I had an episode of Eastenders I was hoping to catch. Maybe I can help, if you let me?" he suggests.

"Nice, mate! How's the Queen Vic? Alfie still causing bloody trouble?" Vex interrupts as I go to reply, and I glare at him as he flushes, dropping his gaze and taking another quick puff on his cigarette.

Christopher looks less than intimidated at this point, and I wonder what the hell kind of Psiren Vex is trying to be. I mean, I know I've been kind of quiet on the torture and threatening front, but he's really crap at it so far.

"Look, I'm looking for my daughter. Her name was Arabella Dragos, born 1591. Don't ask how. I don't have time for questions," I explain, and his eyes widen.

"Okay — give me a minute. I remember that surname." He reaches across the table, and I watch him as he sifts through the piles of books.

"How can you possibly know about each individual person who has died here?" I ask him, and he shrugs.

"I don't. But I do partake in many walks through the graveyards here. I get insomnia, you see. Sometimes names stick. Dragos is pretty unusual." He gives the explanation calmly, and I nod, watching him as I let my pupils recede.

I sit back down in my seat, having gotten to my feet to yell at Vex, waiting in silence for the bishop to speak again.

Vex watches me as he forms one cloud of vile smelling smoke after another, and I momentarily contemplate ramming the cigarette up his nostril for being such a jackass.

After around twenty minutes of tense silence, the bishop speaks, passing me a book.

"Here — Anastasia Dragos." He points out the listing to me.

"No — my daughter's name was *Arabella*," I say fiercely, and he frowns.

"The birth date is the same though — see, here." He gestures to the listing again and I stare at the four letters. *1591.* The year I had lost my life, and she had started hers.

"I told you that's not her! Her name is Arabella! Look again." My whole body goes numb, heartbeat becoming audible in my ears. I exhale heavily.

He frantically searches as I clench my fist atop the table, and Vex frowns.

"Love, is it possible he didn't honour your wishes and named her something else? I mean, he *took* her from you. Perhaps naming her what you wanted wasn't his top priority," he suggests.

Something inside me snaps.

Of course, Jason hadn't named her what I had wanted. He didn't even want me to be her mother. So why would he?

I feel lost. Like Arabella; my Arabella was a figment. She was never real. She was someone else. A stranger—

Anastasia.

"There is no other record of anyone named Dragos buried near here," Christopher informs me, the lines in his face deepening as he fidgets nervously under my gaze.

"Where is it then? The grave for this — *Anastasia*?" I demand, the name disgusting in my mouth. He sighs.

"It's in the graveyard beside my home. That's why I recognised the name," he explains with a nervous yet sympathetic glance.

Vex gets to his feet, and I stand, caught in the moment. Do I want to see the name I hadn't chosen, belonging to the daughter I had never known, etched so permanently upon limestone? Do I want to stand upon her bones and know in my blackened soul the finality of it all?

I've travelled all this way, and yet, now the sense that I've been overcome with ever since I spoke with Poseidon himself, the sense that nothing I do matters, overwhelms me all over again. My pain made new.

I don't have to speak a reply. I don't have to form words. Vex does it for me, pushing me to freefall through the emotional unknown of not just any loss but the loss of a child. My child.

"Mate, just take us to the grave."

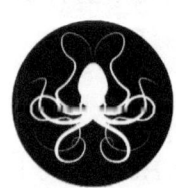

6

A ROSE BY ANY OTHER NAME

THE WROUGHT-IRON GATES, TWISTED into gothic swirling silhouettes, cast shadows upon my face as the crescent moon shines low in the sky. The bishop turns to me as Vex stills at my side, the creases of his face deep and defined in the crisp hue of the night's stark light.

He pushes his glasses up his nose, exhaling a fine mist into the air.

"The grave you seek is right at the end of the central row, in front of these gates. It's underneath the cover of a weeping willow, by the low wall," he informs us, folding his arms across his chest and shivering visibly. I don't feel the cold, and I cannot find it in my heart to pity him either, despite his evident chill.

"Thanks, mate. Oh, and if we find out you've called the police or anything like that, we'll come back and murder you in your sleep. Got it?" Vex voices the threat casually, and the bishop breathes out heavily, staring next at me with a weary expression. I've been silent since we left the library, merely following Christopher and Vex out of the Cathedral, trailing them like a shadow as my heart grows increasingly numb with each step.

Anastasia.

The name is playing on repeat in my mind like a hideous echo. It's not the name I picked, not as beautiful, not as fitting for who I felt like my daughter would grow up to be. I always thought she'd be a stunning, extraordinary woman. A woman who attracted others with her gentle strength, the perfect mix of kindness and courage. She would have been good. Far more so than I ever have been.

The bishop continues to scrutinise me as I check back into the conversation and realise that he probably expects a response from me, despite my lack of intention of giving one.

"You can go now." I don't thank him; it doesn't even occur to me. I don't feel like I have anything to be thankful for at this point. He shattered my vision, which I have hung onto for hundreds of years, effortlessly with the mere discovery of a single word on a single page.

"Come on, love." Vex places a hand on my shoulder and squeezes. I don't flinch away. In fact, I barely feel him as I move with his coaxing and push the wrought-iron gate open. Stepping inside the graveyard, my feet fail to sink into the frozen soil of the ground. The scent of lush vegetation and nearby chimney smoke mix in the air as I take a single step forward, trying to swallow my fear.

"You go on ahead. I'll be right back," Vex assures me, turning and walking away, leaving me alone. I don't follow his path, transfixed by the long row of identical looking tombstones standing uniform, cold and hard in the ground. Sighting the willow that the Bishop spoke of, I continue to tread forward, watching as the leaves shift, rustling. A low cobblestone wall surrounds the graveyard, and on all sides, tiny houses stand, the light from their windows glowing warm, like distant stars, out into the cold.

My breath is sharp in my lungs, cutting the flesh as I inhale deeply.

Reaching the tree, I part the curtain of leaves and step inside its naturally occurring alcove. Turning left, I exhale a sigh, my breath visible in front of me.

In the ground, lopsided and crumbling, it sits. Her gravestone.

Anastasia Dragos. Born 1591- Died 1658.

The stone is barely discernible amongst the shadows cast by the tangled branches of the willow, and only the badly eroded letters of her name, slightly indented into the limestone, give away the identity of the grave.

I'm glad, in this moment, for Vex, not that I'd ever tell him that. Because I realise, despite my claim otherwise, that I never would have found this alone.

I stare at the stone, expecting to feel something, anything. Some wave of grief, some pang of long-lost love rushing back like a bitter, warm tide. Something, anything, yet I feel nothing.

It's just a stone, and I'm still just as dissonant from everything around me as I had been before I came here.

I don't move as the leaves behind me rustle, only slump with a deep exhale. Vex moves in next to me, his shadow melding with mine as it falls upon the frozen earth.

I turn to stare at his face, the lilac of his irises penetrating the darkness of the space as he glances back at me, both of us at a loss for words.

We stand there, staring down at her name together as the wind blows around us, and Vex reaches across to me in the dark, placing something in my hand.

I look down at my palm as my fingers close around his gift, bringing it forward and into the sparse light so I can stare at it.

A single white rose.

"Where did you get this?" is all I can ask, examining the softness of the petals as they caress my fingertips. It reminds me of the silken skin of my daughter, the one and only time I ever held her.

"I, uh — stole it. From another grave. I figure they probably get flowers all the time. You need it more." He looks uncomfortable as he brings up his hand to rest on the back of his neck, averting his gaze from mine. I wonder if he expects me to scold him or make some sarcastic remark, but the only words I can think of spill from me in a flood of unexpected sincerity.

"Thank you."

I bend down, looking at the headstone and cocking my head, trying to feel something, anything. I lay the flower on the dark, rich soil above where she lies, long gone, dead. As I raise a hand to trace the curve of the first letter of her name, the vision takes hold.

It passes in a blur of images, threatening to break me, and as the fog recedes and the vision concludes, I feel something at last.

Regret.

"You alright, love?" Vex's dull yet noticeably anxious tone brings me back to myself as I allow my eyes to refocus on the tombstone in front of me. My hand still hangs, outstretched, over the first letter of her name. Unable to find the words to reply, I fall back onto the earth behind me, letting the frost of it seep through my jeans.

Vex takes a seat beside me, not hesitating to join me on the ground.

"Hey, what happened?" He moves close to me, and I don't pull away, not even slightly as my head hangs and my dark hair falls around my face. He rests a finger on my jaw, tilting my head so my eyes meet with his, and he cocks his head before letting out a small, even breath. "What did you see?" he whispers, voice soft. I blink once, then twice, eyes threatening to fill with tears. I flutter my lashes, refusing to cry in front of him as I harden my resolve.

"I saw what Jason did to her," I explain, and Vex nods, but doesn't ask any further questions. After a few seconds, unprompted, I continue. "So, my daughter was twelve years old when she started getting the one thing from me I was always afraid she would," I express. Vex nods again, sucking in air as his nostrils flare and his cheeks hollow.

"The bloody visions, right?" He guesses correctly, and I nod.

"So, Jason had already told her horror stories about me, of course. Told her I'd been possessed. She was terrified when she started seeing things, so she kept them to herself as much as she was able." I see her face swimming in my mind, the terror in her eyes, reminding me so strongly of Starlet the first time she'd experienced the visions. It makes my heart squeeze, threatening to shatter. Her hair is long and raven, eyes forest green, skin flawlessly tan. She's stunning, even as a child, and the image of her urges me to reach out and touch her, even though she's not really there. I can see myself in her, and Jason too, but it doesn't stop me wanting to stare upon this first clear image of her forever.

"So — how did she end up here?" Vex enquires, crossing his legs in front of him and continuing to stare at me with unwavering and unnerving care.

"She fell in love with a boy when she was fifteen. Told him her secret. As they never do, things didn't last between them, and when it was over he outed her to the entire village. My husband, the hero that he was, tried to send her to the same convent where Starlet was kept, but they were full. However, one of the investors in the place knew of an opening here in England. So, he shipped her here without a penny to her name. She lived out the rest of her life with the church and died—" I'm not sure how I feel about this after I summarise it this way. The overwhelming emotion I feel now is guilt. I could have gone back to find her after I'd turned. I could have tried, could have fought harder, but I didn't.

I twist my fingers into knots in front of me, wringing them and breathing in and out, focusing only on the fact that I'm still living and have no choice but to continue doing so. It's a desperate moment. Yet Vex, somehow, shockingly, lets me know I'm not alone.

"You couldn't have done anything to save her. You know that, don't you? I mean, if you'd have gone back — tried to find her, maybe they would have locked you up too. Besides, you couldn't go out in the sun, it's not like you could have been a mother to her, love." Vex speaks the truth of the matter, the truth I don't want to hear, but surprisingly it makes me feel a little better.

"He didn't even name her what I wanted." I sigh, though I wonder if I should be so upset over something so trivial.

"A rose by any other name would smell just as sweet, love. The name doesn't matter. She's still your daughter. No name can change that. Nothing can. Not even the gods." He's trying to be kind, a friend perhaps, but instead of being comforted, I'm merely frustrated.

"I thought coming here, seeing this, would give me closure, make me feel more like myself. Instead, I just feel the same. I feel empty and trapped in a situation I didn't ask for," I admit. Vex frowns.

"Maybe then it's not the fact you feel you failed your daughter that is causing the problem. Perhaps it's something else," he suggests, licking his bottom lip and blowing a cloud of condensation into the air.

"Like what, oh wise one?" I roll my eyes at him, sick of the sentimental atmosphere and practically gagging to get back to our usual hateful repertoire.

"Maybe you're worried you're going to fail the Psirens." Vex speaks his ridiculous attempt at a theory aloud, and I laugh, unable to help myself.

"Ha. I don't think that's it. I didn't even want this gig." Shrugging it off, I wonder why Vex assumes he knows me. We've barely had more than two meaningful conversations the entire time I've known him.

"And yet, Poseidon gave you the sodding job, anyway. Funny that," Vex muses aloud, and I scowl, partially relieved that he's giving me something to get pissed about.

"What, are you saying I really do want the job? Because that's—" I begin to retort, but he shakes his head.

"Oh no, I'm bloody sure you absolutely don't want the job, the amount you bitch and moan. Though maybe that's the point." He's speaking in riddles, riddles I don't have time for.

"Look, whatever. Either way, it's totally unfair." I shrug, getting to my feet. I don't have time for his totally unwarranted personality assessment.

"You know, I've been thinking, the last person who wanted to use the power of the Psirens for himself nearly got us all killed," Vex calls after me, hurrying to his feet with little grace, as I walk back out from under the willow, turning my back on the grave we've worked so hard to find.

"You — *thinking*? Now there is a novel concept," I quip, sick of his commentary. He had been sweet with the rose and all, but it's not like that gives him permission to psychoanalyse me to death.

"Oi. I'm serious!" he exclaims, storming after me as I pick up my pace, ready to get the hell out of this stupid graveyard.

"Yet another novel concept. Two in a row. Well done."

"Well, maybe you should just stop being a bitch and bloody listen to me. How's that for a novel bloody concept?" Vex yells this time, clearly more frustrated than he's been letting on.

"Excuse me? Why the hell should I listen to you?" I spin on my foot, folding my arms and putting up my highest level of external defence. It's almost as if he cares, and I can't be having that. Over my freaking dead body.

"Maybe because if it wasn't for me, you wouldn't even be here! I did this for you because I don't want to be bloody carbonised by some god when you get us all killed with your careless, '*I don't give a flying fuck*' attitude." He's out of breath as he steps forward, and I scowl, opening my mouth before he picks up his rant right where he left off. "Seriously, love, who do you think you're bloody kidding? You're terrified of failing and taking it out on everyone else. You just hate me because I don't roll over and take your shit like every other bloody person on this planet. You hate me because I actually give a shit about you. Anything real, anything that you can't chop down to making you the victim, to being unfair, terrifies you. Anything which you might actually have a chance to affect, to take responsibility for, to not screw up in the most monumental way possible, scares the living daylights out of you. Because if you fuck it up with the Psirens, nobody is to blame but you, and maybe you are just as irredeemable as you've always believed." He takes a step forward and implores me with his gaze, fury and care melded into something warped and unrecognisable behind the glassy whites of his eyes. "This is in your hands. So, step up to the bloody plate, or get the fuck out of the batting cage. None of us have time for your self-pity any longer. You got a shit stick; we get it. That's life. Get the fuck over it. You're stronger than this." He's pure fury suddenly, storming past me and purposefully knocking my shoulder so I'm spun halfway round on the spot.

I follow his figure with my gaze as he storms out of the gate, slamming it behind him and leaving me standing in the graveyard as the smashing together of wrought-iron rings out into the night.

As I stand still, shocked, perhaps not even by his tone but at the undeniable truth of his words, I look up to the sky as the first flake of snow begins to fall. Holding out a hand, a single flake lands in my palm. I don't feel it. I'm too numb, the truth of a stranger's condemnation still echoing loud in my mind. I stiffen to stone on the spot, every repetition of his words making the truth louder and harder to deny.

7

WRECKED

I SAUNTER BACK IN the snow, which falls slow and melancholic through the festive air of the small English city. I don't feel its chill as it lies upon the roofs of cottages and cobblestones that pave the ground, merely a shadow in the white blur as I head back to the Wig and Mitre.

It's not far, and as I push in on the rustic looking wooden door, the warmth of the place envelops me along with the smell of alcohol and cigarette smoke. My heart falters in its sombre beat.

Vex is sitting at the bar, hunched over the rich mahogany of its adequate length, head hung low, looking down into the depths of a half-empty pint glass. The back wall of the pub is lined with assorted bottles of alcohol in rich hues and is scattered with holly leaves and rank, poisonous mistletoe.

I stride across the tack of the crimson carpet, mapped with cream fleur-de-lis, sitting down next to him on a wooden barstool padded with jade velvet. Reaching into my back pocket, I slam down a fistful of cash onto the bar-top sticky with hops.

"We're checking in," I state simply, folding my hands in front of me and leaning forward as Vex refuses to glance my way. The bartender observes me with interest, lurching forward in a quick and greedy motion to grab the cash laid bare before him.

"Names?" he demands, voice deep and lacking refinement.

"Booking under Fischer," I reply with a sigh, bored with so many formalities. I'm really not in the mood.

"Ah, you were supposed to check in last night," he grumbles. I shrug.

"I'll pay you for both nights; don't worry." At these words, a thick fox-like smile spreads across his face, as though he's not used to someone who finds absolutely no worth in money.

"Oh, well, thank you, Miss." He puts a plump hand over the place where his heart resides, causing the layer of fat coating his skeleton to wobble. The too-bright lights of the bar bounce off his bald head, which glistens with a slick layer of sweat, and his eyes crease at the sides.

"Can I get a glass of red wine, please?" I ask him, desiring suddenly to forget and let go. Something I haven't felt the courage to do in a very long time.

"I thought you didn't drink?" Vex's voice comes over my shoulder in a growl.

"Well, I haven't in a while. But I am from Cyprus originally. I do like my wine, grew up on it," I express, trying not to be visibly affected by his prior outburst.

On the walk here, I realised what angers me more than the fact he's constantly analysing me, is the fact that what he says actually makes sense. Even if I don't want him to, he seems to know me better than I do. It's infuriating, but denying it isn't helping me, either.

"You're not from Cyprus. You don't even speak bloody Greek!" Vex counters, still not making eye contact as he brings his pint glass to his lips and drinks deeply.

"Min ypothéste aftó pou den xérete, maláka" I condemn him, and his head turns to face me as his eyes widen. The bartender places a large glass of red wine down in front of me, which I promptly take in hand and bring to my lips. The scent of it, the richness and full body of the flavour, coats my tongue and slicks my throat as I drink deeply. Vex continues to stare.

"I stand bloody corrected," he relinquishes, and I smile.

"Yes, you do. But you were also right before. About me," I sigh, internally pained by the fact I'm having something slightly resembling a meaningful conversation with someone I quite often want to kill in his sleep. I just can't bear the thought of leaving this place worse off than when I came. I can't have endured this trip for nothing.

"Well, bloody hell! What — did you see Lucifer ice skating to work on your way over here? I think hell just froze over." He's smug as he takes another drag of beer from his tall glass, foam bobbing. I shift uncomfortably in my seat.

"Oh, shut up. I just — I don't want the Psirens to get eviscerated because of me. I have enough guilt already. They're just kids," I sigh, the buzz of the wine hitting me. I guess my tolerance isn't quite what it used to be.

"So were you once," Vex reminds me. I nod, wondering how long it's been since I've felt young and naïve.

"Yes, but they shouldn't have to live with the guilt I live with. If I can save them from doing the things I've done. I guess that's a good enough reason to try," I express. Vex looks surprised as his eyes widen.

"That's the thing. We need to forget about Poseidon. Doing this for him isn't a good enough reason to deal with all the crap that comes with it. You have to do it for you, love."

"You sound like a life coach," I scowl. He shrugs, the rounded hunch of his shoulders rising and falling automatically.

"Maybe that's because you need one," he retorts, and I roll my eyes. He's probably not wrong, as much as it pains me to admit it.

"Look, shut up. You were right before, okay? About the being afraid thing. I am afraid. I don't want other people's lives in my hands. I don't even know how to save myself. That's it," I admit. He shakes his head with a chuckle.

"I think you're missing the point, love."

"And what would that be, oh coacher of life?" I demand, on the edge of my seat as I wait to see what comes out of his mouth next.

"If Poseidon wanted those souls saving, he wouldn't have put you in charge. Don't you see that?" He upends the glass in his hand and downs it to the dregs in one large gulp, gesturing for the bartender, who continues to watch us with interest, to draft him another.

"Well, Poseidon is a moron. We all know that." I take another mouthful of wine, caressing the rim of the glass with my fingertip as I place it down and look into the bloody depths of the glass. I let the alcohol clear my mind, lulling me into a welcome yet unforgettably false sense of security.

"I've had that guy in my head," Vex begins, and I feel myself rolling my eyes.

"Yes, yes, you're so special — mighty vessel — Blah blah blah!"

"Poet and you didn't know it, love." He smirks, then smiles at the barman, lighting a cigarette as he serves him another pint. I find myself inhaling the scent of the smoke as he exhales into the air, a shiver running up my spine at the familiar musk.

"What I meant to say was I got a look into how his mind works," Vex continues, biting his bottom lip and cocking his head as I take a purposeful sip of my drink, the layers of flavour unravelling upon my tongue. Elongating my neck and tilting my head back, my long black hair moves to tickle the base of my spine.

"How wonderful for you. Now, it makes sense—" I lick my lips as I set the glass down yet again, crossing my arms in front of me and leaning forward, looking at our reflections in the mirror behind the bar. If you didn't know us, you could mistake us for friends.

"What makes sodding sense now?" he sneers. I shake my head, a smile spreading across my lips.

"Just the fact you drink so damn much. If I'd had that psycho in my head, I can't deny I'd have gone sunbathing long before now," I admit. Vex chuckles.

"You'd be amazed, the crap in that guy's head. He's having serious marital issues, if you ask me." He takes another puff on his cigarette, tilting his head back this time so I can see the throbbing of his carotid beneath the pale fragility of his throat. He blows smoke up in a vertical column, showering me in the scent of him yet again.

"No shit. This entire war would never have happened if they'd just go to freaking counselling. Hey, maybe you should apply, seeing how you're so full of life's wisdom?" I tease him, and he points to himself with a look of utter incredulity on his face.

"Like Poseidon would sodding listen to me. I might be a man, but a mortal man is the equivalent to dog shit on the bottom of his brand-new shoes. He really bloody hates mortals. Like *really*." I wonder if he's feeling the effects of the alcohol as headily as I am. It certainly seems like it, as we both seem to be dropping our usual vexation in favour of more productive and surprisingly interesting topics.

"I got that impression from him, funnily enough." I shrug. Vex nods, his eyebrows rising on his forehead as he slips his jacket off, placing it down on the bar beside him.

"That's my point. He doesn't give a shit about mortals. Or mortality," he continues. I frown.

"I'm still not seeing this point you insist is there," I catechise him, pursing my lips.

"My point is that he doesn't want you to tame the bloody Psirens, at all. He wants you to direct their rage and power to a suitable target. He chose you to rule them, but it's not because of your lack of darkness or some kind of expectation that you'd become an innocent little sodding angel. You're the only one out of us who can see the ways who you are is wrong. Embrace them, and still control them." He takes another slug of alcohol from a fresh pint before continuing as I listen, actually interested in what he has to say now I've gotten rid of my pride and quelled my defensiveness. The wine has certainly helped. "The Psirens don't need a fair ruler. They need a dictator. It's what they respond to. I saw it with Solustus. He might have used that power over them in the wrong way, but the fear he used to control them with kept them in line." I finish my glass of wine and promptly order another as Vex's words fall over me and I try to make sense of what he's saying.

"So, you're saying I need to play the bad guy?" I query, tone nothing if not surprised. He nods with enthusiasm, as though he's highly stimulated by the entire conversation — though whether it's the topic or the fact I'm actually paying attention, I can't discern.

"Callie and Orion — excuse the comparison, love — rule with kindness, fairness. Psirens are going to look at that and see only weakness. You need to rule with a bloody unyielding iron fist. That's why I know you're the right person for this job, and so did Poseidon. You're one of the most terrifying people I've ever met when you want to be. It's why I like you so much. You've taken no one's shit. Well — until recently." He finishes the sentiment, dropping his gaze to the depths of his glass. I cringe.

"You think I've been taking people's shit?" I ask him, taking advantage of the straight-talking atmosphere between us. Vex lifts his cigarette to his lips and breathes in deep, nostrils flaring, before exhaling with a sigh.

"Don't you?" he asks me, and I consider this for a moment. "The Azure I know would never have let that Hydraball game go ahead, let alone allow that goddamn pipsqueak Celius to live after putting our reputation in the toilet even further with the other pods. The Azure I know doesn't mope in self-pity. The Azure I know —" I interrupt him as I take a sip from the fresh glass of wine that's been set before me.

"Alright, I get it. That's the problem though, isn't it? You don't know me. Not really." I break the moment of connection between us, and Vex smirks, a certain knowingness flickering behind his eyes with smug entitlement.

"Well — we're soulmates, aren't we, love? Or did you overlook that little titbit?"

My eyes widen, and I turn to him, furious.

80

"Fuck off. That's utter bullshit." I shake my head with vigour, denying his claim as utterly ridiculous. Which it is.

"Is it, love? Is it bloody really? Because you know I'm a vessel. I absorb. I absorbed the darkness from Miss Callie Pierce, I absorbed the visions from your sister — what if I absorbed more than that, though? What about if I absorbed the part of her soul paired with yours?" He whispers this in my ear as he leans over, and the smoke on his breath curls around my cheek, making my eyes water as I take in the stench.

"Fuck off." I repeat. He laughs.

"Scares you, doesn't it? The thought you could ever be close to someone. Just for a moment. Just one more thing for life to take from you, right?" He's smug, causing the urge to smack him to rear its head within me.

I say nothing, having no response, down my drink, and order another.

Several hours of silent drinking later, and Vex's resolve cracks. We're both drunk, drunker than we should be, but I really don't care.

"Well, I'm wrecked, don't know about you," he announces.

I snort, giggling.

"So, what's new?" I ask him.

"Oi! That's enough of that shit from you, love. The amount of wine you've had, I'm amazed you're not mounting me right here," he smiles, salacious. I roll my eyes.

"You're such a creep, you know that?" I ask him, still giggling, and he snorts.

"And you're a bitch."

"Well, aren't we a pair? Freaking made for each other." I joke to myself, remembering his insane notion that we're *soulmates*. It couldn't be further from the truth. At least it's insane enough that I can laugh at it, though.

"So, love. Have you thought about getting your spunk back?" He licks his bottom lip yet again. I scowl.

"You know you need to stop licking your bottom lip like that; it's not sexy, it makes you look like a fucking stalker," I snap, angry at this small yet significant feature, which undeniably drives me crazy.

"So that's a no on the spunk then?"

"Yep, that's a no," I exclaim, sloppy, and he sighs.

"Shame. I was hoping to watch you screaming my name later." I turn around on my seat, fuelled by alcohol and beyond vexed by him, bringing my hand up and slapping him around the face in full force.

"Bloody hell!" he exclaims, spinning me on my stool and placing his hand on my knee, grabbing firmly. Shivers run up the inside of my thigh and my breathing quickens in my chest, unwanted but undeniably there. "Look, I get it. You hate me. I annoy the shit out of you. But maybe that's because it's what you need to get you out of this sodding pity party you've been in," he exclaims, accusatory. I glare at him.

"You think you're so smart, *Chase*. But the reality is, you don't know shit. Not about me. Not about the Psirens. I was murdering, *slaughtering*, before you were born, and I'll be doing it long after you're sand at the bottom of the sea." I hiss, rage returning to me unlike anything I've felt for months.

"Your pain doesn't make you special, Azure. I don't know who the hell you think you are, but we all have shit. We all fail people; we all lose people. Not all of us let it kill our spirit though," he whispers, the words intended to hurt me as our conversation hits a new rhythm, becoming a competition of who can wound the other more.

"What would you know about spirit? Yours died the day you became Poseidon's little bitch boy," I bite, taking my wine in hand and downing the glass. The contents push me over the edge, and the room begins to spin.

"I'd rather be a bitch boy than some pathetic, scared little girl. Scared of the darkness within, scared of who she is. Because one day, I'll be free of Poseidon. You'll never be free of the beast inside." I get to my feet, pushing the barstool out behind me as my rage builds even more uncontrollably than usual because of the wine.

"You don't know shit about me. In fact, stay the fuck away from me. I don't need this crap." My heart pounds heavily, excited, as the room continues to tilt and sway.

"I know you're a murderer. I know you love it. I know you want nothing more than to give into every single thing that the darkness wants for you," Vex whispers, face delicious in its mask of wicked intent. I scowl, turning on my heel.

"You can just sit here and ponder what else you fucking know then, *alone*. I'm going to bed." I turn on the spot, done with the conversation, and move over to the bartender.

"Can I have the keys for the rooms?" I ask him, and he nods, passing me both keys in the form of weird credit card type devices. I stare at them a moment, alcohol impairing my usual mental speed as I pass one back to him.

"Give that guy this one. I don't want to be bothered." Not waiting for his reply, I spin, storming past several tables full of men drinking, no doubt beyond what they can reasonably handle.

I see more holly, more mistletoe, hanging overhead as I climb the rickety and uneven staircase. It twists around the back of the bar and up to the top floor, and my feet are heavy upon it.

As I slide my hand along the wooden bannister, I catch Vex's eyes tracing my every motion like a predator. I shudder, unable to contain my disgust. Ignoring him, I refuse to give him the satisfaction of knowing I'm aware of him at all.

Reaching the top of the staircase, I find myself presented with a small, hideously decorated corridor. I look down at the key in my palm. There's three rooms that I can see, and I find my room is the one at the far end of the hallway. I'm glad of this and move forward with haste, craving solitude and the darkness within, with which I will finally be alone. Something I had not thought I'd miss.

I slide the key into a slot beneath the golden door handle and push on the thick, dark wood of the door. Stumbling slightly as I flick on the light, another wave of intoxication hits me. The room is simple. Crimson walls, black carpet and a mahogany four-poster bed draped in onyx velvet. It's decadent, surprising considering not only how the rest of this trip seems to have gone but also how grotty the corridor outside is.

Standing on the threshold of the room, the door closes behind me. I lean against it as the rich woods of the space, paired with the bloody red of the walls, become too much, too hearty. Turning the light back off, I exhale as I stride across the carpet, reaching the matching black velvet of the curtains draping the narrow, frosted glass of the windowpane. It looks out over the Cathedral, and then, as I twist, I see it also has a view of the graveyard where she's buried. I move to close the curtains, and as I do, relief falls over me in waves. Tears come to my eyes, and his words echo out in my mind.

Scared little girl.

You're a murderer.

Your pain doesn't make you special, Azure.

I know you want to give into every single thing that the darkness wants for you.

I allow myself to cry as I close the drapes and fall into the bed, letting the shadows fall over me, letting myself experience the loss of everything I had wanted so badly for my daughter. The main reason I'm crying, though, isn't because of the pain I've carried for years. It's because of Vex. Because he can see through me in a way that I can't explain. He makes me feel bare, makes my wounds raw. I can't hide from him, not in the way I usually do. My usual defences seem to melt at the way he goes right for the jugular, for the truth. He rips off all the Band-Aids without regard for anything other than being honest, and I hate him for it.

I want to live in denial, to not care, and yet, the way he's been mirroring myself back at me lately, he's making me realise that maybe what I am can't be changed, can't be tamed or escaped.

Perhaps I have no choice but to give in and be what I've always been. Perhaps he's right when he says that I was chosen to rule the Psirens not for my kindness, for my goodness, but for the fact I have the capacity for rage that is unrivalled and an ability to make decisions without emotional attachment because sometimes I really just don't give a damn.

I ponder the last few days, the turmoil of it all building inside me as I let salt dry on my cheeks. My fists ball in the velvet of the sheets, wrecked beyond repair, as perhaps I have always been.

After what feels like an hour, I hear a knock at the door. I wonder if I've mistaken the time, if I've cried the whole night away, and it's housekeeping or something. Getting to my feet and parting the dark curtains before emerging into the cold air of the room, switching on a bedside lamp and wiping my cheeks dry of tears. I feel better, more like myself, but something is missing.

My mind is clear, clean, refreshed, and yet, I'm still not angry, still not as powerful in substance as I had once been. I reach the door and take a deep breath, not wanting to give away how upset I've been, before turning the handle and revealing him standing there.

"I'm sorry," is his only sentiment. The look on his face, the way he cares, makes me feel physically sick.

"You were right," I reply, and he blinks once, then twice.

"I — I was?" he asks me, rubbing the back of his neck.

"I am a murderer. I am at war with the darkness inside me. I always have been. Are you happy now?" I cock my hip, angry and on the cusp of sober. I feel myself naked under the scrutiny of his gaze. He comes in close to me, wrapping his arm around my waist. I let him.

"I am; I adore your darkness, love. Your strength. Your rage. It's the most beautiful thing I've ever seen. You shouldn't be so ashamed." He looks down into my eyes and I exhale, bringing up my hand to slap him across the face. My palm makes contact with him, but rather than moving away or flinching, he takes the blow, moving with it and looking down at me with pity in his gaze. Not the reaction I was intending.

"What was that for?" he whispers, not angry, but hurt. My rage builds at his lack of action, his lack of retort, as he grabs my hand in his and clutches it gently. I don't know what to say, what to do. I want him to bite, to give me the relief I seek at being the source of his fury. I just know I need to hurt him, need to destroy him for making me feel this way, making me feel any way when I have so long desired to feel nothing at all.

Digging my fingers into his neck, I ram my lips onto his, sliding my tongue into his mouth and tasting the smoke on his skin. I bite down, letting a dark sanguine allure loose as I devour him, addicted instantly to the surprised pain in his groan and the metallic ash of his blood.

Pulling him across the threshold, I slam the door behind us as we disappear, entangled, into the dark.

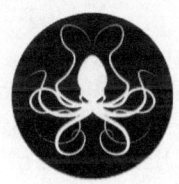

8

SUPERMASSIVE BLACK HOLE

I BREAK THE KISS, ramming my palms into the solidity of his chest and sending him reeling backwards before he slams into the bottom left post of the bed. His eyes are wicked, breathing ragged, and neither of us speak. I merely take the space between us, closing it as I slap him across the face for good measure. I can't have him mistaking this for affection.

Grabbing me around the waist, he pulls me to him. I resist, not to the full of my potential, but I cannot claim total helplessness as my body smashes, flush, into his. The ripple of his abdominals beckons hard beneath his shirt as I grip his wrists. Twisting his hands behind him, I pin them around the bedpost. A smile graces my lips, one packed full of malicious intent.

"You need to be punished — don't you, Vex?" I whisper in his ear, no longer afraid of what's happening between us.

It's been inevitable from the start.

"Oh, *love* — I thought you'd never bloody ask," he growls against my neck as his lips trace me, teeth nipping at my skin. I continue to restrain him against the bed with one hand, both of us standing upright, as I take my hand and begin to caress the solid mass beneath the denim of his jeans. It was immediate as soon as our lips met, and I let my fingernails dig into the plump, firm flesh of him, throbbing beneath my grasp.

He growls, twisting away from my touch and enclosing me on both sides with his arms. Manoeuvring my weight seamlessly into his place, he positions me with rough, clumsy direction so I'm facing the bedpost. My grip on him dissolves now, becoming intentionally flimsy as I lean forward and take the post in my hands.

He brings one palm up around my throat, using the weight of his body and the stiff fleshy tentacle in his pants to push me into the wood. He uses his free hand to reach around, moving it down to my jeans, which he unbuttons within moments before slipping his fingers inside my panties.

I fight it, but a small groan escapes my lips, much to my dismay. I don't want him to know how much I crave this, crave him, and the incredible release my hatred for everything about him will surely drive me to.

"That's it, love — that's right," he purrs in my ear, encouraging my pleasure. As his own breathing becomes ragged, he rubs the length of his erection along the curve of my ass, causing his breath to falter. The noises of both our resistance make the atmosphere between us crackle with self-appropriated heat.

"Mmm. Fuck." I exclaim, breaking his spell over me with my own words as I spin in his arms, the weight of him loosening each time he thrusts against my behind.

"You like that?" he asks me, cocking his head and slipping off his jacket. His biceps bulge in the dark, and his pupils dilate as he brings a hand up to my chin, tracing my jawbone and collecting my hair in his grasp before he gives it a tug.

"Why would you think that?" I bait him, narrowing my eyes as I'm forced to look up at him, licking his blood from my bottom lip.

"You're trembling, love. Trembling for *me*—" he smiles, glee too clear on his cocky mouth. His eyes gleam with arousal, a hundred ghosts of filthy possibilities running through his dirty little mind glinting in the dark.

"It's cold in here." I keep my expression deadpan as he looks at the drapes of the bed with a cocked eyebrow.

"Mhmm. I see. Nothing to do with the fact I make you want to let go, make you want to give into all those dirty little urges that have been niggling at you ever since the day we met?" he insists, taking a step backwards and pulling his shirt over his head before throwing it to the floor. His muscles are cut like ice, sharp, in the cold moonlight dripping in through the gap of the curtains. I lean back against the post, pulling my sweater over my head so I'm stood in just my bra. My nipples protrude through the lace, taunting him.

"My body disagrees with that theory." Biting my bottom lip, a growl explodes from Vex's chest and he practically charges at me. I take a step left before he reaches me, knocking me back through the black velvet drapes. I'm splayed among the onyx sheets within seconds of impact as he kneels in front of me.

I won't let him top me; I refuse, so instead I get to my knees too, meeting him full force in a fusion of kissing and biting, letting blood from his lips and tongue run across my pale skin as he devours my neck with vigour.

"Doesn't look very bloody disagreeable to me, sweet." He brings his hands around me, and I run my long nails down the length of his back as hard as I can. His throat lets sound escape as we struggle in the clutches of this oxymoronic passion, each of us not wanting to let the other know just how much pleasure we're experiencing at the hands of the other.

My rage builds, giving me an erotic thrill as his breathing quickens even further, my breasts pushing against the rapid beating of his blackened heart.

"There's nothing sweet about me," I gasp as he runs his tongue up the side of my neck. Gripping both my hands and binding them behind me, the veins of his biceps bulge blue under the translucent pallor of his skin.

"I bet you taste sweet. Like a sweet, dark, fucking cherry," he whispers in my ear, and I close my eyes, eyelids fluttering as the space between my legs begins to ache. It makes me furious.

I don't want to succumb, don't want to let go, but he's forcing my hand in the most blatantly inescapable way possible.

Holding me down with his weight, he pushes me back to the pillows, taking my bra and ripping it in two so the lace falls, flimsy, from where it's been barely covering the swell of my nipples.

He looks down at me, licking his bottom lip before taking each of my breasts and caressing them in concentrically smaller circles with his tongue. I scrutinise him, not breaking eye contact for a second as his teeth graze me with irritating agony in all the right places. I whimper, gritting my teeth furiously, as I burn for him, the desire to screw him into submission growing with every passing motion of his tongue against my flesh.

Having had enough of his deviancy, I grab his head between my hands and bring my knees up so my feet are pushing against his chest, kicking him back with such force that he rolls onto his back, head hanging back off the foot of the bed, helpless. I grin, heart pounding in my chest as I yank off his jeans in a quick motion and then straddle him, still wearing my own.

I push the seam of my jeans into the hard length of him as he ebbs, hot, between my thighs. His mouth opens into a supermassive black hole of ecstasy, held back only by the restraint he's gathering from the dark power raging within. I run my nails down his neck, scratching and leaving bloody trails down his body as my fingertips descend, tracing the definition of his pectorals, and then abdominals, curving around the deliciously dark v of his waist, where flesh usually fades to tentacle, and grabbing his disgustingly attractive length with both hands. He groans as I pull his foreskin back over the head, fluid spurting from him, and bend down, licking it up and watching as he tenses. A mangled cry of pleasure is unwillingly let loose as the salt of him disperses over my tongue, and I smile, gazing up at him, continuing to move my hand and pleasure him with unrelenting sincerity.

I watch as he bucks like a prize stallion, body straining and helpless as I pin him with my weight, leaning forward and biting gently down on his neck, just above where his carotid pulses with the rush of his lust-filled blood.

"Fuck! You're going to make me —" he exclaims, so I still, removing my hand from him and letting his length fall flat against the tense ridges of his six-pack.

"You bitch!" he curses, sitting up and grabbing me by the shoulders. I smile at him, wickedness drenching me, as I cock my head and purse my lips with the satisfaction of denying him release.

"You want it, come and get it," I purr, reaching down to my jeans and touching myself just to frustrate him further. I let my fingers explore my folds and curves, slick and hot to the touch, as he watches me, starvation lacing his expression.

Hanging my head back in surrender to my intent, I moan, the only sounds audible over my cries being that of him sputtering, his breath coming hard. Desperation audibly poisons each of his inhales as he begins to sound like a rabid, starving dog.

He lunges at me, ripping my jeans off, and I roll back onto the sheets as he had done just minutes before, helpless to the momentum of his weight as he uses my ploy against me. He grabs me by the hair, pulling me to my knees and slamming me into one of the wooden posts of the bed yet again.

"Hold on, or I'll spank you raw," he promises darkly.

"That's not much of a deterrent," I snort, and he brings his fingers up, ripping the underside of my panties wide open as I clutch at the

89

wood before me. I expect him to take me, to bury himself into me and punish me for teasing him so, but he doesn't. I brace myself for the impact of him from behind, but it never comes.

Instead, I feel him pinning my ankles to the bed before, moments later, his tongue slips up into me.

I inhale sharply in surprise, the pleasure too intense as he laps at me, softly opening my hot orifice and trailing down to my clitoris, taking his own damn leisurely time.

"Mmm," he laughs at my surprise, his chuckle vibrating at my tender aching skin, which only becomes wetter as he whispers. "Just like cherries. Black cherries. I knew there was a part of you that was still sweet. Even if it is the most filthy, beautiful part." His words almost undo me as he goes back to working with his tongue, sucking and caressing the epicentre of my surrender repeatedly, until I feel myself ready to empty right into his mouth, delivering the sweet nectar he desires against my will.

I cry out, and my muscles tense as I reach the edge. He stops, running his tongue down the inside of my left thigh, and digging his teeth into my ass with an audible chuckle. I exhale heavily, furious, as I turn over my shoulder and glare at him.

"Two can play at that game, love," he promises, collapsing onto his back and placing his hands behind his head, presenting himself to me. I climb atop him, but he grabs my wrists as I move to bend forward, to take him deep inside and ride him dry.

"Uh, uh, uh." He stills me atop him, and I scowl.

"What? Don't tell me you're not man enough for the job now—" I goad him. He only smirks.

"Oh, no, love. More than up to the task, it's just — I want you to *own* it. Take it like it's your god given fucking right. I'm not going to give it to you. Oh, no. That would be far too simple. Don't you see? I want you to *take* it. Steal it if you have to. If you want it, you work for it, my sweet, black cherry. Let go." He whispers these final two words, sending a shudder through me. I feel my eyes dilate to black; the rage, which I've been denying truly belongs to me, returning full force as my arousal reaches its peak.

I'm done playing games. I'm done fucking around. I just want the release I deserve. The release he's withholding from me like a prize asshole of the deep.

He watches me, a smile of pure, unrestrained pleasure taking over his face as the evil runs loose like a tsunami of desire through my veins, setting my skin on fire.

"Happy now?" I ask him, gazing down at him, superior, as dark lines map my skin.

"I'm about to fuck the most beautiful woman I've ever seen into sodding oblivion. Wouldn't you be?" he asks me.

I observe him from above as his eyes trace my nakedness. I take his hands in mine, running my nails up his forearms before pinning his wrists above his head, stealing what belongs to me, that which he is so happy to withhold.

I look deeply into his eyes as they dilate once again, this time fully, reflecting my shadow and arousal back at me. Positioning myself, I lick my bottom lip and then his before sliding him inside me with a single, ferocious backward motion. He grunts, eyes widening as he strains against my grip. His legs part, trying to taper the sensation and regain control. I lean back onto his thighs, letting his hands go free, knowing he is far too deeply entrenched in me to even think about moving.

Rising and falling, it builds between us again, and I pick up my pace until we're both so far into the dark realms of excruciating ecstasy the world dissolves into that of mere sensation.

It's a pain-fuelled act as it escalates. He bites me, claws at my flesh, curses me and damns me to hell. I feel him pulsating inside as he fills me repeatedly, causing my insides to ache and my flesh to tremble, tender and slick with undeniable yet unwelcome need around him. We both cling on to silence wherever we can, wanting the act to last forever, as we tear at flesh and smash into each other repeatedly and without restraint like a merciless tide during the world's first storm.

In the last moments as he swells, driving himself into me now with a lack of ability to control himself, he causes me to shudder as a final, agonisingly sweet, edge takes over my entire body. It emanates most excruciatingly from my groin, his pelvis grinding against my clitoris. I growl, feral and demented, as he pours his rage into me, scorching hot and deep, only slicking me further and increasing the intensity of it all. I clench around the unforgiving hardness of him and climax, throwing my head back and digging my nails into his pectorals as a scream escapes my lips. I let go in a torrent of rage, pain, and anguish, every muscle coiled for violence.

The darkness runs through me as I work out the ache, grinding into him with sweet, dark vigour. He watches me from below, eyes wicked and victorious as I surrender to not only him, but me.

I collapse to one side, splaying out beside him, my breathing now the only audible sound. Ragged and intense, it brings with it a clarity I have been needing for a while.

I am powerful. I am dark.

And *that* is okay. It's who I am. It's what I need to rule. Just as Vex said.

I look over at him, scared now it's over. I'm worried he'll think it means more than two monsters working out their abominable rage and distasteful desires upon one another to avoid the danger and pain of constant restraint. Vex doesn't lean over, doesn't try to hold me, or kiss me. Instead, he merely looks across and lets his eyes caress my limp, pale form, spider webbed black and blue with the darkness I've been fleeing from for so long.

"So — that killed an hour. What should we do to pass the rest of the daylight hours, my dark, sweet cherry?" he asks, face innocent.

I know his intent is anything but.

As I have lost the war within myself, conceding the battleground of my silken white flesh, now mapped dark once again, so does the sun surrender the sky to the rise of the moon over the horizon. I watch as the dark curtains flutter, revealing the glow of sunset outside the window. I'm wrapped in the drapes from the four-poster bed, which lies now in ruin, splintered wood protruding with phallic blatancy into the air where the posts buckled beneath our never ceasing grind. The bed frame itself cracked in two under the impact of our rigour and violence.

We had not held back, and as Vex lies beside me, lighting up a cigarette, I gaze over to him. He's bruised, scratched, and torn. Bitten and ravaged beyond compare. The tip of the cigarette glows in the dark, illuminating the bruising upon the razor sharpness of his cheeks.

"Nobody can know," I decree into the silence. He looks at me, cocking his slashed eyebrow in obvious disdain.

"Ashamed are we, pet?" he asks. I only nod, not replying as I lean back onto the floor where we're strewn. He sighs.

"Bloody fine then." He's angry, perhaps wanting to display me to the city as a bloody, beaten carcass he has conquered and slain. A hunter

92

returning with the skin of his prey. Unfortunately for him, I am no meek animal, snivelling around in the dirt. I am a queen.

I am a queen.

The thought reverberates through me like the aftershocks of an earthquake that has been stirring beneath the surface for quite some time. The walls of my denial have fallen to the ground at an act that has liberated the darkness within, and now I am left staring at the rubble.

So now what?

Do I climb it? Stand upon it and look out over a horizon I have been shielding myself from all along? Or do I rebuild, reclaim the safety of ignorance as my own?

"We should get going." I get to my feet, pulling the drapes tighter around me.

Vex snorts.

"Oh, and *now* she's modest. Don't bother, love. I've seen it all up close now; there's no going back." He's snide, obviously hurting, so I relax my arms and let the drapes fall to the floor, exposing the canvas of pain and pleasure we've spent hours creating in its full glory.

"Happy now?" I ask, not angry, merely tranquil as my mind settles more than it has since the day Poseidon declared me Queen of the Psirens. Everything seems so clear now I've used Vex to un-stopper my own darkness, to practice letting it loose without letting it control me.

He doesn't reply, just gets to his feet and starts looking around for his clothes. He throws my bra at me, pinging it off his thumb with a malicious glare. I catch it, but realise it's been mauled beyond wearability, so simply throw it into the trash can. As I do so, I notice it's the only piece of décor in the entire room that we haven't damaged.

Apart from the bed, the wallpaper has scratch marks and holes where desperate fists have driven forward, seeking release through the torment of the pleasure I've caused. The carpet has been stained in many places with blood and other bodily fluids. The bedside tables have collapsed beneath my weight, and the lamp atop it was smashed within moments of our third time around.

We finish dressing in silence, and I sigh as I realise my underwear is completely ruined. Vex smirks as I slip on my jeans, commando, before taking several steps over to the window and pulling the curtains apart to reveal the twilight.

I stare out over the graveyard, knowing that perhaps this trip wasn't about her at all. It's been about me. My fear, my denial about who I am. My lack of understanding of how to be the ruler everyone expects of me. It's a harrowing thought that I may now be more equipped for a job I'd not even wanted. And yet, I cannot help being relieved at the prospect of no longer having to restrain myself like a caged animal.

I keep my back to the room as I hear him leave, slamming the door behind him in unwarranted fury. After all, he got what he wanted. We slept together; he got to possess me, be it only fleetingly, for one night. Isn't that what he's been alluding to with his dirty jokes and inappropriate innuendos? Maybe I'm a disappointment, not that I care. I had a good time, and now I'm ready to return to the city and deal with everything I've been trying to run from.

I float once again above the black crystal of my balcony, looking down over the city and pondering the journey home. It had been quiet, not so much as a harsh word or even the whisper of an argument the entire drive back. When we reached Whitby and ditched the car, if you can indeed call it that, Vex had taken off into the water, leaving me to make my way back alone. I was glad of his departure, and took the time to think not about what had happened during our stint in Lincoln, but rather to contemplate how I'm going to proceed with the Psirens

I haven't seen him since.

An insecure woman would be all: '*Oh is it me?*' '*Did I do something?* '

But I'm not an insecure woman, so I'm really finding it hard to care.

I proceed back into the suite, to where I've set up a large black crystal table. Atop it, wax coated maps of the area lie on its flawless surface, weighted with rocks.

I ponder why the surrounding sea is so barren compared to other locations and yet recall somewhere that might be perfect for what I seek. I need to train the Psirens myself because handing off the job to someone else will not earn me their fear or respect. And yet, I will not be under the scrutiny of the other pods while I do so. My methods may indeed seem unorthodox, but the Psirens are too, so it really is necessary.

I hear a knock ring through the water and sigh as it reaches me, hoping above all things the person behind it doesn't possess tentacles.

"Come in!" I call, twisting in the water to face the door, which opens to reveal not Vex but Orion.

Fine, I'll take it. I exhale a flurry of bubbles as my brother swims into the room, his royal blue tailfin shimmering blatantly behind him.

"What do you want?" I demand, staring back down at the charts in front of me as he approaches the table, not wanting to look him in the face.

"I just wanted to see how you got on during your trip. I saw Vex — he looked a little, well, *beaten up.*" His lips quirk into a half-smile as sentiment leaves them, and my head snaps up as I move to glare at him.

"Yeah, so what? He got mauled by a bear. That's all." I make up the lie on the spot and Orion nods slowly, eyes widening in disbelief.

"A bear? In England? They don't have bears in England," he informs me, his smile growing wider by the second.

"We went to a zoo," I add, face deadpan. He shakes his head.

"I see. How was it?" he demands. I scowl at him.

"Well, it would have been better if we hadn't been driving around in a shoe box with wheels. So, thanks for that, bro." I cock my head at him, and he laughs.

"I said a Classic British car on the phone to the rental company. I have no idea what that even means. Vex told me to say it." He narrows his eyes, and I return his sly gaze.

"A likely story." I snort, and he rolls his eyes. "And the cigarettes provided with no lighter?" I enquire, and he smirks this time. "Oh, that was definitely me," he admits, eyes sparkling, and I shake my head, dark hair blossoming around me in the Pacific's warm salt.

"Three freaking hours with him, in that car, with no lighter — and you're supposed to be the righteous one out of the two of us. I think that might be bullshit." I force my expression to remain calm as my eyes focus on his stupid, perfect hair, as he curves, coming around the side of the table.

"Did you find her grave?" he asks me, and I nod.

"I did. It wasn't as healing of an experience as you all promised. Still glad I went though, I guess. I got to threaten a Bishop and everything," I explain. #

Orion snorts.

"How wonderful for you."

"How were the Psirens while I was gone?" I demand. Orion looks shifty beside me as he runs his fingers through his hair.

"I think the other leaders have a lot more respect for you than when you left three days ago; I'll put it that way." I can't help but smile as he continues to seem uneasy.

"Nobody got hurt, did they?" I ask, internally hoping Isabella got what she deserves.

"No, but I think it's safe to say you have your work cut out for you. They don't respect anyone at this point. I mean, the fear from Poseidon's brief visit is all but lost in their memories now. We're all concerned." I stare at him and smile, confident for the first time in ages.

"You don't have to be. I have a plan." He's surprised at my words, staring at me with his kind, pale blue eyes and shooting me a smile with his too-white teeth.

"You — have a plan? Does that mean you're actually going to rule them?"

"It does. Not like I have a choice. But I owe it to them to stop them from living with the regret I do. I also owe it to myself to try. I've never really done that before. I just kind of — gave in to fate, I guess. Living with visions, it's easy to forget you have the power to choose." I speak the words, sounding wiser than I feel, as Orion puts his hand on my shoulder.

"You should come with me. I have something to show you." He is proud of me as he speaks, mouth upturning in the corners as his gills open and close, letting bubbles loose every few moments in an uninterrupted stream.

"Is it a Ferrari?" I ask him, hopeful. He rolls his eyes.

"Not for all the bananas in Barbados," he replies. I faux pout, vowing to myself that one day I will procure a Ferrari and drive it without crashing.

He leads me over to the door of my suite, opening it and pushing me forward slightly.

"NOW!" he yells down the corridor, slamming the door shut behind me. From the end of the hall, blood thirsty Psirens with dark eyes erupt in a small pack. They race toward me, trapping me in the dark confines of the crystal hall.

As they reach me, I feel them bind my limbs and cover my head with a sack of some kind, taking my vision from me. I panic, caught totally off guard, wondering if while I was gone they realised I have no idea what I'm doing. That they know I'm a fraud.

As they carry me through the water, much to my continuous protest, all I can think is, *what now?*

9

A BLOODY BORING AFFAIR

I'M BLINDFOLDED AS ORION pulls me up out of the water and onto a cold, stony surface. I phase automatically from Psiren to mortal form, feeling my legs return to me as I ponder how fast they can carry me far away from here, wherever here is. The bag has been removed from my head, which I guess is a plus because I really don't do well playing prisoner, as I'm sure the Psiren's carrying me will attest.

All I've been able to hear the last half an hour is Orion's irritating repetition of the words, "Calm down. Jeez."

If he could have seen me rolling my eyes every time, he probably would have shut up, but the bag and the restraining by a mass of rabid teenage killers kind of made this an annoyingly moot point.

"Orion, this is ridiculous. Why am I blindfolded? If Isabella wants to publicly behead me for her own amusement, the least you could do is allow me to glare at her in disapproval as it's happening," I growl.

Orion laughs as he wraps me in what feels like a towel. I cling onto it, sick of this charade already.

"Oh, shut up. Now, follow me, and be careful; the staircase is steep." He pulls me by the hand as I notice a lack of heavy breathing and the prickling sensation of eyes upon my back, indicating the Psirens who had transported me here have left.

We journey up a winding staircase, my feet slippery against the stone as Orion guides me, and I wonder momentarily if he's walking me off the edge of a cliff or something equally stupid.

Warmth envelops me, and the scent of bergamot and burning driftwood fills my nostrils. My feet meet with velvet and then more stairs as I ascend them, calves burning. Orion continues to pull me blindly forward without pause, irritating me immensely.

Shortly after, I hear the creak of an opening door, and I'm shoved forward. The audible locking of it behind me makes me roll my eyes again, sure that if I wanted to, I could just kick it down.

Several moments pass as I stand there, debating whether to remove the blindfold myself before it falls from my eyes at the hand of none other than Mrs. Callie Fischer.

"What are you doing here? Wait, where am I?" I'm startled as I look around at the room, finding not instruments of torture or an audience awaiting my death but racks of dresses, along with panels entirely formed from mirror-glass. They show the two of us standing alone in three-hundred-and-sixty-degree intensity.

"You're in the parlour at the Lunar Sanctum. Haven't you been here before?" Callie asks, looking surprised as her perfectly plucked eyebrows rise on her forehead. I glare at her, expression dripping with disdain.

"Do I look like the girl who spends hours preening to you?" I demand. She smirks, pushing her hair behind her ear nervously.

"Why do you think I had you kidnapped?" Giving a sly, self-satisfied smile, she turns away from me. I examine her as she goes, dressed in an aqua silk robe — a colour she's obsessed with. Her tanned legs protrude flawlessly smooth beneath it as she steps toward one of the many vanities, pointing at its constituent chair.

"Sit," she commands, sure of my compliance.

I look at her with confusion.

"You brought me here for *a makeover*?" I query, the idea ridiculous. She grins, causing violent urges to rise in my chest. I haven't been wrestled all the way here, blindfolded, so I can have my freaking *split ends* taken care of.

Right?

"No. I brought you here to be crowned Queen of the Psirens," she explains, and my heart stills a moment before picking up its punishing beat. My rage dissipates, and I sigh.

"Why on earth would you want to do that? Nobody wants me to be queen. I'm not even sure *I* want to be queen," I admit, biting down on my bottom lip as the truth of my words fills me with relief. Callie laughs as though she's closer to my age and not merely a child.

"You think I did? Want this, I mean?" She cocks her hip, and I frown.

"Of course you did. I see you with your perfect blonde hair, smile, and all the other leaders looking at you with actual respect. You were born for this crap," I condemn her. She snorts.

"Are you insane? Like, *actually* insane? Because you know I didn't ask for this either. The only difference is I stepped up, and you have yet to do so. And you know, you're far more equipped for this job than I ever will be. You're far older than I am. You know the seas. You're strong as hell. You know, I — I *envy* that in you. The way you don't give a crap. The way you're so sure of who you are." It's like she's talking about someone else as we stand, face to face, fraught and exposed. She's staring up at me with conviction in her eyes, extinguishing the otherwise plausible notion that she's merely blowing smoke up my ass.

"Then it would seem we're both wrong in our assessments." I relinquish my prior assumptions, running my fingers back through my damp hair and wrapping the towel around me tighter. At my awkward motion, Callie moves over to a pink pouf sat in the middle of the plush carpet, grabbing a black silk robe and throwing it to me.

"Yes. I know I may seem like I have the other leaders' respect, but I'm terrified they'll see right through me. I don't know what I'm doing either." She admits to her fear of inadequacy as I slip the robe over my shoulders, pulling my hair out of the collar and tying it around myself. I frown.

"So, you've invited them to watch me put on some hideous monstrosity of a gown and stand on ceremony? What, you think that'll convince them I'm really domesticated?" I ask her, and she smiles.

"This is a private event. It's not about the others. It's about you and the Psirens. They're your people, and they need to see you as their leader. I planned this whole thing myself. It was my idea. So, before you think it's some trick, it isn't. You alone bear the responsibility of being queen. You also deserve the same respect, and that starts with this ceremony. It's partly my fault with the other rulers, I'll admit. I haven't been putting my fin down with them because I was worried they'd think I was biased. Then it occurred to me. *They're* the ones who are biased. If it weren't for you, we'd all be dead. It might be easy for them to forget that, but I know I haven't." She finishes her little speech, and against my better judgement, I cock my head, narrowing my eyes as my temper recedes to embers from my less than orthodox arrival.

"You're not wrong. They are biased. Not that I can totally blame them. I don't even know if I can control the darkness within myself, let alone the others. I mean, I'm getting better at it, but I still have miles to go before I sleep," I breathe, moving forward to the chair and taking a seat. Crossing my long pale legs in front of me, I stare at myself in the mirror.

"It's a complicated situation. But they don't see it how I do. The Psirens may very well be our most powerful asset if handled correctly. Things may be calm right now, but there will always be another threat just over the horizon." Callie looks sad and I wonder what it is she's referring to, though I can't bring myself to ask. Silence falls between us momentarily as the young, not so innocent, queen runs her hands through my hair, looking over my shoulder and into the mirror with fondness. She's not Starlet, but she's still the closest thing I have to a sister, which I guess explains why she pisses me off most of the time. It's true, nobody can push your buttons like family — unless, of course, they have tentacles and a cocky British accent.

"I'm not wearing a freaking monstrosity, by the way — and nothing pink," I announce, giving in to the concept of the event itself.

"Oh, trust me. I learned my lesson in the Arctic about trying to make you wear pink." Rolling her eyes, which sheen with unspoken amusement, she twists her mouth, taking in my reflection and pondering my face.

"So, you have a dress?" I enquire, and she nods.

"Yeah, I designed it myself." The words fill me with dread as they ring out, high pitched and laced with enthusiasm. If it's aquamarine in colour, I'm going to strangle her with it.

She stands behind me, continuing to run her fingers through the thick dark strands of my hair like I'm only a kitten.

"Well, are you going to show me the stupid thing, then?" I bark, and she jumps slightly, as if I've interrupted a thought bubble which has been forming too slowly in the desolate space between her ears.

"Yeah, I have it on a mannequin here. Give me a second." Abandoning me in front of the mirror, she stalks the length of the room with square shoulders and head held high, opening a sliding door leading to a closet on the far wall. She pulls out the dress form, which is covered in a black silk sheet, setting it in the middle of the room before pulling it back. I take in the dress, cocking my head from left to right before looking at her.

"Well, I suppose it's not *hideous*." I smile at her, impressed despite myself. She gives me a wicked grin.

"I thought you'd approve."

I do.

What do you know? The girl did good.

Considering I actively contemplate slathering Callie in tar to prevent her own fashion sense from frying my retinas daily, she really hit the nail on the head with my entire look for this event.

I'm wearing a black, floor length wrap dress, elegant in duchess satin, and yet flattering in an elongated mermaid silhouette. It's got a spiked, bustier top, pushing up my breasts and slimming down my waist, with a slit up the front of the skirt, exposing as much bare leg as possible. My hair is insane — perfect for me, but insane. She's back-combed it into a faux hawk, which makes me appear feral and wild, with the long locks that usually hang past my ears braided tight against my skull. Slipping a hair clip resembling silver coated seaweed into the back of the up-do, which has been teased and gelled beyond what I had ever contemplated being able to sit still through, she takes me in, satisfaction clear in her features.

"You look—" she begins, but I finish the sentence for her.

"Badass?" My mouth twists into a grin against my volition as the black lipstick, highlighted with a matte azure sheen in the centre, spreads wide, exposing my white teeth. My eyes are surrounded by black and accented with the same shimmering blue, and I let my pupils dilate dark, thick eyelashes fluttering, as I give her the full effect.

"This dress, it'll change when you enter the hall," she reveals. I give her a questioning glance.

"It's not going to make fireworks shoot out of my ass, is it?" I demand, paranoid at once. She shakes her head.

"Uh — no," she relinquishes, passing me a pair of shoes. I sit down on the pouf behind me, the wildness of my hair tickling my bare spine. The puddle train of the gown pools around my ankles as I slip on the first sandal stiletto. They are Grecian in look, climbing my calves to the knee. Black in design, they boast a silver fish's skeleton as the centrepiece of the straps.

"You really put a lot of thought into this." I stare up at her as I slip on the second shoe and fasten it to my foot. She blushes, fidgeting on the spot.

"I just feel you deserve the same treatment as everyone else. If nobody else was going to make it happen, then I said to Orion that we would." She seems embarrassed, and I don't do emotional scenes unless that emotion is rage, so I cough a few times before changing the tone of the conversation.

"Well, you made me look fabulous. Though you had a great starting product, so I'll deduct props for my natural pizazz," I tease her. She shrugs, fighting the flush creeping across her cheeks..

"I knew you'd never come if we told you beforehand. I'm glad you like it. I wasn't really wanting to force you down the hall towards Callista." She gives a small giggle, pushing her hair back behind her ear yet again. It's loose and curly, and her makeup is toned down and natural. "I better get dressed." She shuffles past me as I stand again, staring at myself, indulging vanity in the floor-length mirror.

"So Callista is doing the ceremony?" I ask her, and she nods.

"She requested to perform it, and I didn't see why not. She really likes you." Callie shrugs as she pulls on a black floaty blouse and some, surprise, surprise, aquamarine sequined pants. They'd be fabulous in black, as would most of her clothes.

"Did you ever see this happening? Me being a queen?" I ask her, feeling suddenly raw as it occurs to me I'm about to step into the shoes of someone I never thought I'd be.

"Actually, now that you ask, it makes perfect sense to me you would be," Callie replies without pause. I snort, rolling my eyes.

"Bullshit."

"Not bullshit. Truth. I won't lie. What's the point? If you fail as a queen, I'm the one who will suffer. I'm married to your brother, and I'd have to deal with the consequences if he lost you, not to mention what would happen to the Psirens. I mean, what would we all do without Vex's undeniably crucial entertainment value?" she asks me, and I smile against my better judgement, heart rate picking up slightly at the mention of his name.

"Yeah, I've had my fair share lately," I remind her with a grimace. She shakes out her legs, righting the way the sequins fall upon her thighs as they shimmer in the light, too resonant of her tailfin.

"How was it? The trip?" she asks, and I open my mouth to respond, but she continues after a pause. "I saw Vex. He looked like he'd been beaten up. Barroom brawl?" she assumes.

I cuss internally.

Damnit, why didn't I think of that?! I came up with— mauled by a bear? Smooth, Azure.

"Yeah, sure. Can we go now?" I ask, glossing over my reply as she puts on a single teardrop moonstone necklace before giving herself a final once over in the mirror. Her springy ringlets glow golden, a halo of goodness in contrast to the abrasive darkness of my own.

Silent, she unlocks the door of the parlour and sets me free as I stare out onto the landing before travelling its breadth. Leaning over the dark balustrade, my head hangs, taking in the staircase's length. My gaze is instantly pulled into the shadow where the double doors, the exit to the Lunar Sanctum, reside. I wonder if she expects me to bolt, to run, and then realise she's probably put me in heels to prevent that from happening.

I guess this has always been inevitable, so I step forward, wearing shadow from head to toe, inside and out, always.

I'm not making this into a big deal, as I'm sure it had been when Callie and Orion were crowned. Not that I'd know. I was happily late to that event, and I certainly made an entrance.

"Well, are you going to open the freaking doors, then?" I bark at Orion, who looks exasperated as he stands in a black suit with a black shirt and tie on underneath. I'm definitely sensing a colour theme — though what, exactly, escapes me. Callie takes my hand in hers.

"You nervous?" she asks, face full of excitement for me. I cock my head at her, expression remaining serious.

"No. Let's do this shit and get it over with; my panties are chaffing," I bite out. She nods at me, stifling a laugh and taking several steps forward. She and Orion open the double doors to the hall, revealing me to the room and the room to me.

I expect to be blinded, but I'm pleasantly surprised to be staring into shadow. The entire hall has been transformed from shimmering white and deep crimson, with floors mapped through with gold filigree vines, to black and cavernous in its unending darkness. Ceiling to floor, the entire place is pitch black, until suddenly, as Callie claps her hand, the entire place erupts into the splendour of the deep. Bioluminescent décor illuminates the space within moments like a wicked and tempting milky way I'd like to drown in. The runner, lined on either side with azure fibre-optics, lights my way down to the stage at the end.

As I step through the doorway, dark eyes turn to me, each body dressed in black suddenly coming alive with neon, glowing accents to keep them visible in their enormous shifting mass that's otherwise cloaked in darkness.

They scrutinise me, and as I hear an audible inhale, I look down at myself, trying to seek the source of their fixation. My dark gown has come alive in the shadow, peppered now with thousands of azure specks of light. Looking back over my shoulder, I see the puddle train flaring out behind me, a galaxy trapped in a wave of duchess satin.

Edged with the azure glow of the hundreds of stars left in its wake, it laps against the shores of my immense depth as I take a single step forward.

Well, that's — unexpected.

I turn back to look down the length of the runner leading to the stage and feel their eyes on me collectively, waiting for something. I wonder if they expect me to smile, to blush, to act bashful under the weight of their collective abyssal gazes, but I don't. This is my damn coronation, and I'm going to own it like the queen I'm about to be.

I strut the length of the runner, legs protruding from the slit at the front of my dress as I proceed to the sound of primal drums toward the stage. The drapes are spotted with bioluminescent stars too, and as I get deeper into the black-lighting, I realise that the smell of bergamot and burning drift wood is coming from incense burners smoking in the corners of the hall.

My eyes dilate fully, allowing me to take in details that would be lost on others. I search for one particular face in a crowd, coming up empty, much to my relief. I take the stairs in my stride and come face to face with Callista, who smiles at me with that eerily serene expression that makes her look as though she's lost in a dream. She's wearing a long black robe that glitters, falling in asymmetry across her body, draped with casual perfection.

"Please kneel," Callista requests. I shake my head.

"I'd rather stand, thanks. Let's get on with it." I'm bored already; not one for ceremony, formality, or anything resembling either. I want it done and dusted as fast as possible.

"Callie and Orion asked me to perform the short version of this ceremony — I cannot imagine why." She looks at me, the alabaster of her pupils unsettling. Her thick lips pull into a half smirk, half disapproving smile as she turns from me, moving to pick up two wicked objects from the throne behind her. She holds one out to me, a sceptre made from whale bone carved with ancient looking runes and wrapped in black pearls. Next, she drops a heavy orb into my palm, a tennis-ball sized black pearl encased in a cage of black diamonds. It's cold to touch and reflects my bioluminescent make-up back at me in a dull hue.

"Repeat after me," Callista exhales, her voice soothing even though I can feel the scrutiny of hundreds at my spine.

"I, Azure, Mother of Psirens," she begins, and I snort. Is she joking? That's what they came up with for my title? Is this some kind of cruel, unintentional irony? I turn back to stare over my shoulder down the length of the aisle to Callie and Orion, who stand stoic, slightly amused twinkles exuding from their crystalline irises out into the dark.

Rolling my eyes at them, I turn, rushing my way through the words as if I'm only ordering a drink at a local bar.

"I, Azure — Mother of Psirens—" I bite out and contemplate yawning, but then I wonder how my people would feel about that. Maybe they'd see the funny side, or maybe they'd all just up and leave. Either way, it could be a good thing for me personally, if not for the future of the Psiren race.

Callista glares at me with a firm hard line for a mouth, imploring me to take this ridiculous spectacle seriously.

"Solemnly vow to uphold the values and protection of the people of this world. To tame the darkness and to direct its unprecedented power on earth to the service of The Circle of Eight and my fellow council members. To place the needs of my people before those of myself and to understand that my life and death belong to the service and wellbeing of my God and his mission on earth." The vows leave me feeling nauseous at the thought of pledging my subservience to any god.

So, I cough.

"How about — I solemnly vow to do my very best for the Psirens in my care, whether that be taming their inner darkness or allowing them to truly embrace it for the greater good of those around them?" I query her, not content with vowing something I'll never uphold. I look back over my shoulder at Callie.

"Good enough?" I call back down the length of the hall, and I watch as her hand comes up to cover her face in exasperation. Orion nods beside her, trying not to laugh as he gives me an over-enthused thumbs up. I turn back to Callista. "Go on—" I gesture for her to hurry, still clutching the orb and sceptre like spare parts of a machine I have no clue how to fix.

"If you'd like to take the throne." Callista steps aside, allowing me to examine the chair for the first time. Made from charred, black driftwood, it's covered in crustaceans and urchins which give it a jagged and completely intimidating outline even in the dimmest light. I turn, sitting down upon the hard grain of the surface and crossing my legs casually as they protrude through the slit in my skirt, exposing my pale flesh to the crowd. I hear whispers from the Psirens as Callista moves to collect the crown from a small table beside us and narrow my eyes. Looking out into the crowd, I find not respect, but the lacklustre attention and mocking gazes of bloodthirsty teens.

I stir, leaning forward and finding Celius in the crowd, turning to a blonde Psiren beside him and smirking up at me. It irks me, and as I watch the mass ripple with similar disobedience, my Psiren rage returns full force.

Callista places the crown on my head, a concoction of charred black wood, bones, black pearls and sea urchins intertwined with tiny veins of blue light. It's heavy against my skull, painful even as the urchins dig into my flesh, but I barely feel it; I'm too busy seething upon my jagged throne.

"I present to you, blessed Kindred of Poseidon, Queen Azure, Mother of Psirens. Please bow to receive your new ruler." She gestures for me to stand. Sceptre and orb still in hand, I rise and survey the crowd beneath me. They don't kneel or bow, or even so much as stir. They merely snigger like the adolescents they are. As I watch on, I place the sceptre on the floor, discreetly untying the straps of my sandals, though it doesn't matter as hardly anyone is paying attention, anyway. Picking up the sceptre yet again, I square myself, glowering.

The weight of the responsibility I have to them kicks in, and as any good mother should, I realise it's time I teach right from wrong and how to respect their goddamn elders.

Tightening my fingers around my sceptre, my eyes zoom in on their many faces as a full and wicked smile spreads across my face, leaving it gaping with the possibility of violence. I kick off my shoes beneath my skirt, ready once again to make a giant scene at a public event. I should seriously consider charging at this point.

As I launch myself from the stage with a sudden and feral sounding growl, the crowd jumps, receding from me as if I'm a ferocious tide eroding their resolve, taking a few steps back in surprise. I hear Callista gasp slightly as I stalk forward, my skin mapping dark with power as my muscles unfurl. The tension in my body is mine to manipulate as I wish.

I find him still sniggering in the crowd, the one I need to make an example of.

My steps don't falter as I raise my arm, swinging the length of the sceptre across his face and knocking him onto the floor. The Psiren's part, not doing what I have partially expected and mob attacking me, but merely watching on with interest.

Celius' muscular torso strains beneath my weight as I fall to my knees on top of him, taking the mass of the dark pearl orb in my left hand and smashing it into his face. His eyes widen with fear as my nails abandon their clutch of the orb, allowing it to roll, bloody, across the floor with a high-pitched ring. Wrenching back my hand, I ball it into a fist and bring it down into his face, hearing an audible crack as it strikes his jawbone and blood rushes to my knuckles. He tries to fight back, but I've got him pinned to the floor from the waist down with the positioning of my legs, a move I used on Vex not so long ago.

When I grab his wrists as they come up to throttle me, he smiles, wondering what I'll do now I have no remaining limbs adequate to beat him with. I smile back at him, lips pulling back over my teeth.

I don't speak, merely lunge for his throat, digging in my incisors and breaking open the creamy pallor of his neck's flesh like a casket of red wine. The blood flows quickly from his carotid, and I drink deep and hard, the heat of it rushing through me and my heartbeat deepening as I take in his life-force. Once I'm done, I rise from his body, which lies bleeding on the floor beneath me. My face is covered in his blood, and it drips, hot, sticky, and delicious, from my lips and off my chin before trickling gently into my cleavage.

"I believe Callista said you should fucking kneel!" I bark, looking around at them, as I plunge the end of the sceptre through Celius' skull, eviscerating his brain and causing him to die right there. I look down at him like he's trash. Then, stepping aside, I kick his limp body with my sandal to make sure he's well and truly dead.

As I do so, a tidal wave of fear move through the room as the Psirens bend at the knee and kneel, bowing their heads. The room is silent, not a breath audible in the air, which crackles, alive with my authority. Callie and Orion stare at me as I survey the sea of Psirens. They both nod, satisfied.

I don't smile. I merely clear my throat.

"Training starts at dawn. Now, follow me. It's time to rave," I decree, watching as they get to their feet in silent uniformity. Tossing the sceptre to the floor and giving one last look over Celius' dead body, I stride back up the length of the hall.

Callie and Orion open the double doors, and Callie stares at me with wide yet unmistakably proud eyes.

"I — I had a reception all planned," she whispers, disappointed.

My face is still bloodstained and mapped black and blue, but I smile at her, sure I must look monstrous. However, I'm also sure this may very well be the truest reflection of myself I've ever presented to anyone.

"I'm taking them to the deep. They need to blow off some steam before we start training tomorrow. I'm taking them out of the city. My methods aren't going to be orthodox by the standards of the other council members—" I explain in a quick, clipped manner, impatient as the Psirens clump behind me as I block the door. They could go around me, but they don't; they still, waiting for my next move, pleasing me immensely.

"Alright. I trust you." Callie nods for me to leave and I take off without further word, not sure what I can say that will mean anything.

Besides, I have more important jobs to attend to.

Storming out of the double front doors of the Lunar Sanctum, I lead them, a long line of lost boys and girls, to the edge of the cliff where I had once teetered so close to the ledge with another.

"Jump." I order them, face stoic as I refuse to turn to them, to acknowledge them as people. I want them to earn my respect, my attention. I want to teach them to be obedient, and that starts right now.

Underneath the stormy mass of the sky above, I stand, glowing and bloody as the Psirens strip down behind me before running and launching themselves, fully nude, off the top of the cliff. They soar through the air, one by one, silhouetting against the sky, only discernible as the grim moonlight catches the jagged edges of their arching forms.

"So, how was it?" I hear a voice call out as the final Psiren leaps into the waves below, phasing just before hitting the surface with a hard splash.

I spin on my heel, taking him in as he lights a cigarette. A leather jacket adorns his torso, which I know remains marked by me, beneath.

"If you'd have attended you'd know," I retort, and his eyes widen as he catches the red of Celius' sticky blood coating the bottom half of my face even still.

"This really isn't my scene. Bloody boring affair if you ask me, love. Though, the after party — that's something I can get down with." He takes several steps toward me, closing the distance between us. I take a step back.

"Do you remember the last time we were on this cliff?" I demand, and he smirks.

"I do. I predicted you were ripe and ready to be picked. And how right I was," he purrs. I scowl.

"What happened before — it can never happen again," I snarl, and he smirks.

"Oh, fuck off. You and I both know that is a load of utter poppy-cock." He grabs me around the waist and pulls me back away from the edge. The scent of him, the cigarette smoke, the salty musk — it brings back the memories of that night, causing desire to pool unwillingly between my thighs.

"Vex, it's over," I whisper. He grins, predatory, down at me.

"Oh, love. Even you don't believe that. You can't even muster the power to say the words with any conviction." He takes the cigarette from between his lips and throws it to the ground, although it's far from finished.

"Stop," I plead, victim to my lack of restraint. I've let the floodgates open when it comes to him, and now I know how delicious things between us can be. I've had a taste, and now I can't forget it, can't resist it. As if he's become the darkness I've been fighting, embodied.

"Say it like you mean it, and I will," he growls, eyes wild with lust, as I pretend to struggle in his grasp. I purposefully pull away, raising my hand in the air and bringing it down to slap him just like I've always done as the urge to hit him clutches me. This time he catches me by the wrist, slamming his lips down onto mine and tasting the dried blood on my skin.

The dark night blankets us, and I moan into his mouth, heart beating wildly in my chest as his hand crawls down my spine and pulls down the zipper of my dress. It falls to the ground, exposing my undergarment beneath, a single lace thong. He promptly rips it asunder, tossing it to the ground. His fingers dig into my ass as we stand, clutching one another, stuck in a limbo of utter lust and undeniable hatred.

The wind whips around us as he breaks the kiss, gasping for air. His eyes wash over me, making me hate him, hate how desperately I want to find release with him one more time. The rage inside me is too much to be contained for so long again, and for a moment, with him, I felt like I was the one in control of the darkness, not the one being controlled by it.

I gaze up at him, biting my bottom lip and getting a malicious thought.

Perhaps I can have what I want. Use him to find relief from the building abyss inside. After all, I am a queen. But I'd never just let Vex have me so easily. I'm the kind of woman you chase and catch, not the kind of woman who falls to her knees at any opportunity.

"Call me," I breathe against his ear, leaning forward as I turn on my foot, pushing off the rigidness of his pecs and stepping out of my dress before bolting toward the edge of the cliff. I take the plunge, soaring off the ledge as the chill night air quenches the simmering fire he's left sizzling beneath the surface of my skin.

Hitting the surface of the water, I plunge deep after my children, after the Psirens, leaving Vex alone on the edge of the cliff as he had once done to me. I feel the water against my skin as I slice through the sea, calling me into the deep, as it has done for many years. Now, though, for the first time in forever, I swim with intent, with purpose.

Now, I will carve my own destiny, and I fully intend to vex a certain tentacled asshole every chance I get along the way.

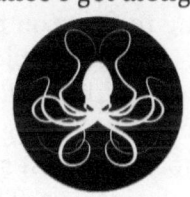

CREEP

VEX

SHE'S A SODDING PILL.

Bitter to swallow, fighting me all the way down my gullet before falling unwillingly into my core and dispersing her dark, dominating tendrils, addictive within seconds. The release of her into my system has the blood screaming inside my goddamn veins, my dick throbbing hard against the front of my jeans like something possessed. I'm aching throughout, in withdrawal, as I raise a hand, shielding the flickering flame of my lighter from the immense wind coming off the sea that lies unrestrained below.

Extinguishing my lighter as the end of my fag catches and lets off a puff of fragrant smoke into the air, I inhale heavily, taking the smoke inside of my lungs and trying to focus on the relief I know is coming at the next exhale. My heart is doing the bloody tango behind my ribs, causing me to stand on edge atop the cliff.

Tilting my head back, I exhale, seeking relief, but finding none. I close my eyes, letting the moonlight cast shadows over my skull, and take in a breath, this time of night air. The aroma of salt, mixed in with the lush greenery surrounding the Lunar Sanctum behind me, is overpowering to my Psiren senses, but it's not what I'm seeking. I grasp what I'm craving in my nostrils, letting them flare and enjoying the scent of her, fleeting as it might be. Sweet, dark cherry ignites a fire in my synapses, causing my mouth to flood with saliva and my stomach to tighten with desire.

The smell takes me back as I keep my eyes closed, the cold of the wind whipping around me and providing much needed contrast to the fire beneath my skin.

The arch of her flawlessly smooth back, a bead of sweat falling between her shoulder blades, sharp with need, and down into fragrant dew which coats the top of her ample ass. I remember the feel of my fingers plunging into the tense knots of her muscles, seizing flesh that hadn't been touched without cruel intent for years.

Bloody woman. I curse internally.

I open my eyes to the black of the sky, but I don't see it. I see the dark silk of her hair falling flawlessly over her swollen breasts. The sea is no longer a shifting mass of water but the quivering of her body atop me as she takes what she wants without permission or pause, each cresting wave another undulation of her pleasure, locking me in and rippling around me.

Bloody — Pissing — Sodding — Woman! I growl, taking yet another quick inhale of my cigarette and finding myself so angry at the lack of relief for my usual cravings that I throw the barely touched fag to the ground, stamping on it and leaving an overdramatic dent in the earth.

I think back, wondering if I felt like this the night I'd been turned. Alyssa's embrace had been deceptively bloody loving, of course — but it hadn't felt like a curse. Azure felt like fire from beginning to end, like what I was doing was dangerous beyond what I knew. I'm realising, only now, that I've potentially become addicted to something with someone who has no desire to repeat the act, or so she claims.

I'll be making sure it's not a one night only kind of show if it's the last thing I do — I vow, tensing my jaw and acknowledging the ridiculous hunger I've acquired for the act itself.

Is it her? Or is it how I become when I'm with her?

Who goddamn knows?

I've had sex before. Good sex, lots of it. And yet — what happened in the dark of that hotel room, spreading from the internally cast shadows of the shit we've been infected with — it was something bigger than me. It was primal and raw, and it was also the biggest thrill of my life. I have never felt that alive. Not riding a motorcycle at top speed, drinking myself stupid, or injecting pleasurable chemicals beneath the skin.

She was something else, has always been, and yet for some reason she can't see it. She's too bloody melancholic, too broken in her own mind to see the powerhouse I see in her.

She's a Queen alright, a bloody dark demon spawned right from the undercarriage of hell to torment me from now until the day I sodding die. Alyssa warned us, said we were damned, but I never figured that meant I'd be cock-teased by some wild, dark goddess trapped in mortal flesh until I was ready to drown in the weight of my own frustration.

Is it hell? Or bloody heaven?

Who pissing knows!

I turn my back on the ocean, walking away from the ledge on which Azure and I find ourselves teetering so very often, not only physically, but metaphorically. I can still hear her as I do so, the sound of her climax ringing in my ears like some resonant haunting from the demons we had not exorcised but exercised that night.

It can't be the last time. It just can't.

Over my undead fucking body.

She says I'm a creep, that I'm dirty minded and base. Is she wrong? Hell no. But maybe it causes her so much disdain because I'm everything she is, too. Where I wear the face of a dark killer with swagger and undeniable cool, she's too afraid to.

I don't understand her. I mean, I can pretend to, and there are moments when I look at her and catch the ghost of an emotion I recognise from a book I read once. But I'm sure that she's ashamed of who she is, and I'm bloody certain she's ashamed of who she became underneath the sheets with me.

She acts like the weight of the world falls upon her and her alone rather than knowing, as I do, that we are merely pieces in a much larger picture. I have surrendered to the idea that the current will take me where it wills, and yet she resists, a fighter through and through.

I don't know what will happen now. I know what I think I want to happen. I want to lock myself in a room with her and give in to the carnal urges riddling through me, cancerous and destructive to both of us.

I do know one thing for sure though, and that is the fact that she has the sodding power now.

As much as I may bloody love to hate it, it is me, not her, who is vexed now.

Bloody hell.

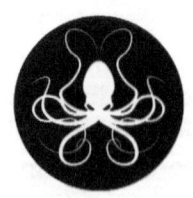

A CHRISTMAS TAIL

KAYLA'S SURROUNDED BY GEOFFREY, Stan and Theodore, snuggled deep down into her brand-new mermaid blanket. It's been a long day, Christmas day to be exact, and the evening even longer.

Callie, Orion, Gideon and I had all been invited for a late Christmas dinner, and having nothing better to do, I agreed to come. I haven't been the best sister, having had no opportunity to Christmas shop, but Callie and Orion have, unsurprisingly, more than made up for my lack of anything resembling care by gifting her a tiny, pearl-thread tiara, which she's refusing to take off. If only she knew the true weight of the icon upon her head. Would she still wear it so readily?

Probably. I mean, she seriously loves anything shiny.

"Did you have a good day, Kayla?" I ask her, and she nods.

"Yes. I love my tiara. Did you get any nice gifts, 'Zure?" she asks, and I think back to earlier today. Vex had given me three orgasms in an abandoned cave before dinner, catching me off guard and naked as I had come ashore to meet up with Orion and Callie — but I guess I can't tell her that. Or anyone. It's too goddamn weird that I've fallen into that dark pit of despair more than once since the first time it had happened. I still can't seem to make myself stop though, as much as I completely and utterly detest myself and everything about him every single time it's over.

"Nah. I'm a bit old for gifts," I express with a small smile, and her mouth twists into a tiny, thoughtful pucker. I reach behind me to straighten the blue silk of my blouse and her eyes widen, as if she's expecting something from me. I instantly feel guilty, my soft spot for her increasing in diameter with every single meeting.

"I'm sorry I didn't get you anything," I apologise, as silence falls between us, trying to fill the gap in the conversation with anything other than her questions about whether I have a boyfriend and if he's *dreamy*. It's a no and then a NO, on that front, in all senses of the word.

"That's okay. There is only one thing I *really* want." She's devious with her cute moments, I'll give her that, as she places a thumb in her mouth and begins to suck. Her eyes are wide as her tiny feet wiggle under the comforter, and I roll my eyes, laughing despite myself.

"What is it, tiny extortionist?" I sigh, and she giggles, removing her thumb from her mouth.

"A bedtime story." Her eyes are laced with mischievous intent.

"I don't really do the fairy tale thing—" I grimace at the idea of filling her head with utter rubbish.

Happily ever after and handsome princes? I snort.

I'll save that for Callie.

"No! Not that. I wanna know about mermaids." She eyes me, biting her bottom lip and smiling, as if she does not know that what she's asking for isn't allowed.

"Kayla — you know that's against the rules," I breathe, glaring at her, and she puckers her lips, squishing up her tiny nose.

"I'll find out, you know. I'm smart." She watches me, gaze holding mine and imploring me to tell her everything.

I exhale heavily. I don't want to get into a fight. I've had enough of that with Vex. It's like now he's taking my excess rage from me and quelling my frustrations, I can focus my dark power any way I choose. It's exhilarating, taking me back to when Titus had helped me reach my highest point of intensity as a killer.

"If I tell you, just this once — you can't tell anyone else. It has to be our secret." I give her a stern look, and her entire face lights up in the orange glow of her bedside lamp.

"Really?" she looks beyond excited, and I can't help but smile.

"Yes. Really. I mean, if you want to find out, then you will. It's a bit late for us to keep this from you." I admit the truth I've known these last few months. The thing is, if Kayla wants to find out about Mermaids, she will. She's too mixed up in the world of the Occulta Mirum and its queen not to.

She snuggles down into the covers even further, and I rise from the bed, moving to the door and closing it so we won't be disturbed.

Sitting down on the edge of the mattress yet again, I cross my legs, feeling a peace within myself I haven't for a while. Things are changing; that's for sure, but I'm also feeling more at home with myself than I ever have before.

Taking a deep breath, I cast away thoughts of the last few days and look Kayla straight in the eyes.

"On The Higher Plains, among the Gods and Goddesses of the sea, who constitute the rulers of the heavens, is where our tale begins—"

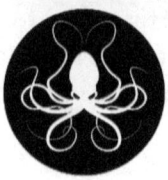

ALSO BY

Queens of Fantasy Saga Reading Order
(As Suggested by Kristy Nicolle)
PLEASE NOTE:
The Tidal Kiss, Ashen Touch, and Aetherial Embrace can be read as individual 3 book stories, or in order as part of the saga.

PART ONE- THE TIDAL KISS
#1 The Kiss That Killed Me
#2 The Kiss That Saved Me
#3 The Kiss That Changed Me

PART TWO- THE ASHEN TOUCH
#4 The Opal Blade
#5 The Onyx Hourglass
#6 The Obsidian Shard

PART THREE- THE AETHERIAL EMBRACE
#7 Indigo Dusk
#8 Violet Dawn
#9 Lavender Storm

CONCLUDING NOVEL
#10 Queens Of Fantasy

QUEENS OF FANTASY SHORTS AND NOVELLAS

TIDAL KISS SHORTS AND NOVELLAS
Beyond The Shallows
Waiting For Gideon
Vexed

ASHEN TOUCH SHORTS AND NOVELLAS
Death Blooms
A Touch Of Smoke And Snow

AETHERIAL EMBRACE SHORTS AND NOVELLAS
Ambrosia Nights

EXTRAS
Infiniflash Fiction Volume One

OTHER GENRES FROM KRISTY NICOLLE

DYSTOPIAN ROMANCE:
Something Blue- A Dystopian Romance Standalone

POETRY:
I Am Arcana- A Tarot Inspired Poetry Collection
Starsong- A Zodiac Inspired Poetry Collection

To keep up to date with the latest release dates, spin offs, and exclusive
content, head on over to kristynicolle.com

ABOUT THE AUTHOR

30-Year-Old British Author of Award-Winning Indie Fantasy Romance, Kristy Nicolle is escaping the pain of Ehlers Danlos Syndrome by crafting intricate and immersive worlds for her readers. She lives in Norwich, Norfolk, with her long-time life partner Mark, and can often be found writing in her local coffee shop - *Botany and Beans*, with a peppermint mocha, surrounded by beloved witchy paraphernalia and plants she knows only too well she'd kill at home.

FOLLOW KRISTY ON SOCIAL MEDIA OR FIND HER AT
KRISTYNICOLLE.COM